Saline District Library
3 4604 91008 6718

Murder in Stratford

Other Five Star Titles
by Audrey Peterson:

An Unmourned Death

Murder in Stratford

As told by Anne Hathaway Shakespeare

Audrey Peterson

Five Star • Waterville, Maine

This novel is a work of fiction. Names, characters, places and incidents are either the product of the author's imagination, or, if real, used fictitiously.

First Edition
First Printing: March 2005

Published in 2005 in conjunction with Tekno Books and Ed Gorman.

Set in 11 pt. Plantin by Ramona Watson.

Printed in the United States on permanent paper.

Library of Congress Cataloging-in-Publication Data

Peterson, Audrey.
Murder in Stratford : as told by Anne Hathaway Shakespeare / by Audrey Peterson.—1st ed.
p. cm.
ISBN 1-59414-273-4 (hc : alk. paper)
1. Hathaway, Anne, 1556?–1623—Fiction. 2. Great Britain—History—Elizabeth, 1558–1603—Fiction.
3. Shakespeare, William, 1564–1616—Fiction.
4. Stratford-upon-Avon (England)—Fiction. 5. Authors' spouses—Fiction. 6. Married women—Fiction.
7. Dramatists—Fiction. I. Title.
PS3566.E765M88 2005
813′.54—dc22 2004062493

Murder in Stratford

Table of Contents

Chapter 1

EARLY DAYS

i

He wasn't always a faithful husband, but come to that, how many of them are? After the first years, he went off to London, leaving me in Stratford-upon-Avon with the kids. Some people snickered and some felt sorry for me, but what do they know about how things really were? There was many a twist and turn to the story before we got to the end, I can tell you.

I'm an old lady now, past three score years, and one day something happened that showed me how wrong people can be. One of those London scribblers came here to Stratford to talk to me. Will had been in his grave some years, and this chap seemed to think Will was what he called an "untutored genius" and that I wouldn't really know much about him anyway, since he had been in London for much of his life.

Of course, he was keen to know about the murder.

"Your husband was once arrested on a charge of murder, was he not?"

"Yes, but the charges were dropped."

His little eyes gleamed with malice. "But the case has never been solved, has it? Can we be really sure . . . ?"

That did it. The fellow was a conceited popinjay, and I sent him on his way. I wasn't about to tell him how it all ended. Afterward, though, it struck me that what he had said wasn't just his own opinion, but probably was what a lot of people outside of Stratford must also think. I've noticed what happens when men become famous. It's always other men who write about their lives, and they don't always get it right, but does anyone ever ask the wife? A woman would tell it straight, both good and bad. And that's when I decided I would write about our lives the way they really were. We have a word for this that we got from the French: it's called a *memoir,* and that's what I have done.

ii

First, I have to tell you about the murder, because many people still think it was never solved. The truth is that we did finally learn who had done it, and I had no small part in that. In fact, Will said I was a "detective" because I was the one who figured it out. But there were reasons why we never made it public.

It had happened one summer night at a large party in our house in Stratford. Many of the guests strolled out into the garden along the paths that wound through the shrubbery and under the trees, when suddenly we heard a shout and learned that the body of a man had been found dead in a far corner of the garden. It was our old friend and neighbor, Richard Quiney, and he had been stabbed with a dagger. Tall, handsome Richard, with his gorgeous red hair and his oozy charm. Richard had never been one of my favorite people, and by that time there were a good many of our friends and family who had plenty of reason to feel that the world might be a better place without him, but it was nevertheless a shock when it happened. Richard and Will had grown up together in Stratford and their fathers were lifelong friends. Somehow you don't expect a man to be murdered just because a lot of people don't like him.

But once you've heard the story of our lives, you'll see what led up to the murder, so we'll go back to the beginning.

It all started one day many years ago when I went into John Shakespeare's glover's shop in the high street in Stratford to place an order for my father. I was in my twenty-sixth year and ought to have been a matron with a family by that age. That this hadn't happened was nobody's fault but my own. My mother, before she died, had tried her best to get me to take one of the local chaps that wanted to wed me. Since my father was a prosperous yeoman farmer in the village of Shottery, near Stratford, they no doubt hoped for a good dowry, but I wasn't taking.

Anyhow, there I was in the shop, and young Will Shakespeare, the eldest son, came forward to take my order. He gave me a bold look that surprised me. The gangly boy that I had scarcely noticed had turned into a fine-looking young man with an air about him that made me take notice.

Young Will wasn't sure of my name. "That's Hathaway Farm at Shottery, is it?" His voice was pleasant, deeper than his age would suggest.

I gave him my order, and he gave me a searching look. "I'll bring them out to you when they are ready," he said.

I knew that he could have sent someone else from the shop and why he was coming himself, and I was amused at his boldness.

And so it began. He came with the gloves. I gave him a

mug of my father's ale and took one myself. We sat in the arbor under the oak tree. It was in the month of May, one of those days when the sun burns right down and warms you through so that the shade feels welcome. He never tried to make polite conversation but plunged right into telling me his problems and his feelings as if he already knew me well, and all the while, his eyes went all over my body. He studied my hair and my eyes and my arms that were almost bare because of the heat, and his gaze went down to my waist and along to my feet and back up to my bosom, and that's where he liked to look best.

He told me how he had been glad his father had sent him to the grammar school. Not many lads had that chance, and he had done well there. The schoolmaster said Will was his star pupil and he wanted him to go to university and study to be a schoolmaster himself.

"Wouldn't that be a fine thing?" I asked.

He frowned. "I know it's a position of great respect and of good pay. The trouble is, I can't see myself spending my life teaching a lot of grubby boys their Latin and their Greek. You see, I want to go to university just to learn more, to read about things I don't know about yet. But my father—well, he won't hear of the expense."

I knew from general gossip that John Shakespeare had once been richer than he was now, that there had been rumors of money dealings that went wrong, and that he was reputed to be close with his purse even in his better days, so I wasn't at all surprised at what Will was telling me.

However, I said nothing, and Will went on to tell me how much he hated being in his father's shop. He had reached the age of eighteen, and he wanted to do something important with his life.

He came again a few days later and found me in the

garden, reading a newssheet. "I didn't know you could read, Anne," he said, looking pleased. Since there were no schools for girls, his surprise was understandable.

I said, "I followed everything my brother learned in the primary school, and made him teach me. Since then, he seldom reads, but I do."

"I see." He told me his favorite author was Ovid, and when I said I didn't know Latin, he promised to bring me a copy of some of the stories that had been translated into English.

That visit had caused my father to ask if the lad was courting. "A bit young for you, my lass, isn't he?"

I laughed and agreed with him. I had no wish to marry anyone, let alone young Will Shakespeare, entertaining as he was. Since my mother died, I had kept house for my father and brother, and we got on well enough together. Not many women had so good a life.

Of course I married Will in the end, but for a long time I had been determined never to marry, although no one knew why. To understand that, you have to go back to what happened when I was seventeen. Stephen Brent, the farmer whose land lay next to ours, needed someone to look after his invalid wife while he was out in his fields. Poor Margaret Brent's body was all twisted up, with knobs on her hands and knees. She had hobbled about for some years, but now she could not walk at all and was confined to her bed. Various women from the laborers' cottages came in to do the rough work, but my job was to supervise the house and look after Margaret. My father, well-off as he was, never passed up a chance for more income, and Brent had evidently made him a generous offer. As for my mother, she consented only if it was clear that I was a lady and not a "servant." Always a stickler for propriety, she gave her approval when Stephen Brent assured her that all the rough work was done by the women from the cottages on his land and I would be mistress of the house.

I liked being at Stephen Brent's place from the first. Instead of being at home, with my mother carping at me, I was in charge of the household. Poor Margaret Brent was too ill to take any interest. Her mind was affected as well as her body, and most of the time she just lay there, murmuring prayers and humming little tuneless songs. Sometimes she was in pain, and I gave her sips of the syrup that eased her.

At first I went over every day and came back at night, but soon Stephen asked for me to stay over when he came in late, and gradually I stayed through the week and went home on the Saturday to be home for church on the Sabbath.

I slept upstairs in a fine bed, though not so splendid as Margaret's. Long ago, when Margaret could no longer go up the stairs, Stephen had brought their best bed down to a large room on the ground floor. It was a standing bed, beautifully carved, with elegant hangings, fine linens, and embroidered cushions. He had arranged a small bed for himself in an adjoining room, to be near her if she called out in the night. This seldom happened, though, as the apothecary had prescribed a strong sleeping draught that gave her nights of painless sleep.

It must have been several months after I started there that something happened that terrified me. Stephen was getting ready to leave in the morning and had gone in to say goodbye to Margaret when I heard their voices raised. She seemed to be pleading with him and he was refusing her—something he rarely did. The door was ajar, and I peered in and saw him holding up a picture in a gold frame. At first I saw only that it was a beautiful painting of a woman, with rich colors in her gown. Then I saw the golden halo on her head, and the truth struck me like a blow. It was an icon of the Virgin Mary!

I gave a gasp, and Stephen, seeing me in the doorway, stared at me with fear in his eyes. I stepped back, he closed the door, and in a moment I heard the sound of a click that seemed to come out of the wall.

Presently Stephen came to me in the kitchen, looking troubled. "I'm sorry you saw that, Anne," he said quietly. "You see, Margaret still clings to the old ways, and she has so little to comfort her. She wants to have the little shrine at her bedside. I've tried to explain that it is dangerous, but she doesn't understand. She says it wouldn't matter if they punished *her,* but you see, I am the one they would take away. And if I went to prison, what would become of her?"

I wasn't the weepy kind, but I felt something making my eyes blurry. I said the one thing that I knew he wanted to hear. "I'll never tell anyone, Stephen," I said. And I meant it.

I never did understand why people cared so much about one kind of church or another. It was all the same God they worshipped, but care they did. From what I heard, it all started when the old King Henry, father of the present Queen, broke off with the Pope in Rome because he wanted to divorce his Spanish Queen, Catherine of Aragon, and marry Anne Boleyn, the mother of our Queen Elizabeth. Up to that time, there was only one church, so everybody was what they now call a "Catholic." Then it seems there were important people who protested against a lot of things that went on in the church, and so they called them "Protestants." You'd have thought that people could have been whichever one they chose, but it wasn't that way. In order to keep power, the King had to make everybody be a Protestant. They closed all the monasteries and then the ones known as the Puritans made all the churches destroy their beautiful images and carvings, and they had to whitewash over the paintings on the walls and make the churches plain. This was supposed to make the people concentrate on the sermon and not be distracted by worldly things, but of course it didn't work that way. Worse than the loss of their images was for many people the loss of their priests. Many of these escaped over to France and down to Spain and even into Italy where the Pope lived. Very wealthy families sometimes kept a priest hidden away, but harboring a priest was a serious crime if they were caught.

In the end, however, people do come to accept the way things are. Just as this was beginning to happen, who should come to the throne but old Henry's daughter Mary, the daughter of Catherine of Aragon, the Spanish Queen that he had divorced. Mary was still Catholic like her mother, and she wasted no time bringing back the old ways. Now people could take out the images they had hidden away or buried in the garden. Some of the priests came out of hiding, and many of the Puritans were persecuted and tortured the way the Catholics had been before. This state of affairs lasted only about five years, and then Queen Mary died and her sister Elizabeth came to the throne and put everything back to where it had been, with the Protestants in power. And that's the way it was when Stephen took the icon away from his wife.

"You see, Anne," he said to me, "Margaret doesn't understand the way things are."

So it was that one day I stopped Stephen as he started out toward the fields.

"Not many people come here to the house," I said.

"Couldn't Margaret have her picture when no one's about? I could hide it away if someone comes."

Stephen gave me a look of astonishment I'll never forget. "Would you do that, Anne? You might be in danger yourself."

"I would be careful," I said firmly.

And that's what we did. In the afternoons, after the cottage servants had gone, I put the gold-framed Virgin on the table by Margaret's bed, and the glow of joy on her face was worth ten times the risk. She would pray and murmur to it, and she seemed to suffer less from the pain. If I had to leave the house, or if someone came to the door, I put the icon in the secret compartment in the wall by her bed, hearing the click in the paneled wood, where not a trace could be seen.

I can see now that that was when Stephen began to notice me more, although it was a long time before I was aware of it. When I turned eighteen, he told me he would be age thirty soon, and that seemed old to me, almost like my father. When I began staying overnight at the farm, that's the way I thought of him.

Then one day my mother asked me if Stephen ever bothered me. It took me a minute to understand what she meant. Then I laughed and said no, he was too old for any of that.

First she nodded. Then she said, "Just the same, Anne, you watch out. He's a fine-looking man and his poor lady can't be a wife to him. You don't want to spoil your chances for a good match."

I suppose I had been aware that Stephen was a handsome man but I hadn't thought about it till then. Which goes to show you should be careful about planting ideas in the minds of young girls.

Now I saw how strong yet trim was his body, how softly

his brown hair lay in waves, how beautifully his eyes glowed like the deep blue of the jewel in Margaret's picture. And now I was aware how often he would gaze at me and quickly look away if our eyes met. Now I would feel my heartbeat quicken when he stood near me. And so it was that when, one evening, he came to me and put his arms around me, I raised my face to his as if it was the most natural thing in the world that we should be standing thus, while he kissed me and murmured words of affection.

What I wasn't prepared for was what happened next. He leaped back, with tears starting out of his eyes. His voice choking, he cried out, "Oh, Anne, forgive me!" And he went on about how wicked he was and how he'd tried not to think of me in that way, and would I forgive him, and so on.

I assured him it was all right, and that night I lay in my bed upstairs and puzzled about things I had never given much thought to before. Of course I could see his problem. It was wrong to love someone other than his wife, and if she had been healthy and normal, it would have seemed wrong to me too. Of course the church said it was wrong regardless, but I hadn't heard the gossip of my mother and her friends without learning that that didn't seem to stop a lot of people from doing what they wanted.

Nothing happened again until one night in the winter when there was a terrible storm. The Brent house was a fine, big house like my own, solidly built to withstand any weather, but on this night the wind was so wild that the shutters banged and a huge branch of a tree crashed against the wall outside my bedroom. With the curtains drawn around my bed, I lay shivering, listening to the storm, when I saw a hand part the curtains and Stephen's face appeared.

"Are you all right, Anne?"

I put out my hand and drew him in beside me, and he

came without protest. We whispered words of love to each other, and after awhile I learned the wonder of bodies coming together in pleasure. He stayed a long time, and we held each other and talked softly about all sorts of things. He told me about his childhood, about how he loved Margaret from the time they met, how her illness was a sorrow to him. I talked about my mother and her schemes for me, and about my father and his love of money.

The next day, I feared Stephen would go on about how we ought not to have done what we did. Indeed, he looked at me sorrowfully when we met in the morning, but not a word did he say. A long time went by, or it seemed long to me, before one night he came again and it was just the same as before, only more full of wonder for me, because no one had ever shown me such tenderness before. My mother was what people called a "good woman," but she was never soft. Her voice was harsh, and she frowned at me often but seldom smiled. As for my father, his ways were brusque. He referred to my mother and myself as the womenfolk and paid little heed to either of us, beyond his meals and his comforts.

So you can see how I came to love Stephen so desperately that my whole life was entwined with his. I often lay in bed longing for him to come to me, and when he went on about how wrong it was, I simply said, "You have given me the only joy I've ever known, Stephen. I can't believe it's wrong."

Over the next two years, we gradually grew at ease with each other, loving and trusting without the need for words, the way I supposed husbands and wives did if they were lucky enough to be congenial together.

One day in the early summer of that second year, something frightening happened. A clergyman came to call. The old vicar had died and been replaced by this young man who held strictly Puritan views. When poor Margaret saw his clerical collar, she cried out, "Father, Father!" and made the sign of the cross with her poor gnarled hands.

I tried to tell him she was not right in the head, but he ignored me and said he would submit the case to the bishop.

Soon, however, that worry was swept out of our minds, for that was the year the plague came again to our part of the country. It had been some years since a bad bout had come our way. Sometimes a few cases turned up, but this one took dozens of lives by the time it was over. It was odd how country people are always shocked by the plague when it comes. It was common to fancy that it was only the big towns like London that were unsafe.

There was never any sense to the way people fell victim. Of course, the very young and the very old often died, but so did perfectly healthy people. Nor did it always go through an entire household. One or two might go and others not. The ones that tried to say it was God's will had a hard time of it, because some of the worst miscreants survived and some of the finest persons were taken.

At first, I was seized with fear, but as the weeks went on, a strange feeling came over me that we would all be spared. So it was with a shock of surprise that one day I found Margaret burning with fever. Stephen bent over her, sobbing. On the same day, I was sent for to go home, where my mother had caught the disease and died within a few days.

Soon after that, I heard men talking with my father, and one said, "*Stephen Brent!* Poor chap. The wife died and now they've taken him to prison."

"What had he done?"

"They say he was harboring a priest. When the wife was

dying, she wanted a priest. It seems Brent knew where one was hiding and brought him to the house, and he was caught."

Horrified, I waited for a month for news of Stephen, and then the word went through the neighborhood that he had died in prison.

I felt as if I had been turned to stone. Then the pain came. I thought I would die of it, but you soon learn you have no choice. Daily life goes on.

Six years had gone by when Will Shakespeare came along. I had kept to my resolve not to marry. And so it was that I came to enjoy Will's visits but had no wish to take him seriously.

The problem with that was that Will didn't see it that way. I tried to discourage him, saying I was too old for him and that he should pursue one of the pretty young girls in the village.

"Oh, they are so silly," he would say. "You are never boring, Anne."

One afternoon, to escape the heat, I had removed my housegown and lay on my bed wearing only my petticoat and camisole. I had dozed off when I heard a sound and opened my eyes to see Will standing beside the bed.

"You look so lovely," he whispered.

Half asleep, I smiled at him. "How did you come here?"

"No one was about, so I came to find you."

He took off his boots and came to lie beside me. "You know I love you, Anne."

I yielded to him because it was infinitely sweet to feel alive again, to feel warmth and affection and the pleasures of love.

Of course he came often after that, expressing his love with enchanting bits of poetry that seemed to spring from his lips without effort. My eyes, my breasts, my hair, my face, all were compared in the most fanciful way with objects of nature, making me laugh. He clearly loved being in love, reveled in having found someone he considered worthy of his adoration. He poured out to me how he longed to go to London, where he would find a life more exciting than anything offered in a town like Stratford. We would be married and I would come with him on this great adventure.

I regarded it all as the passing fancy of a very young man, when events overtook us. My father died quite suddenly. Two months later, I realized that I was expecting a child, and Will was elated. Now the decision was made for me. I knew that I didn't love Will with the intense passion I had felt for Stephen, but I was truly fond of him and happy at the prospect of having his child.

And so it was that on the 28th day of November in the year 1582, William Shakespeare and I became man and wife.

What sort of life did I expect? I was never one to worry much about the future, but I suppose I vaguely pictured an ordinary life in Stratford, but always lively with Will around. I certainly didn't expect that Will would become rich and famous and that we would be involved in plots of treason and murder, but that's what finally happened.

iii

All that was in the future, though, and our lives started out in quite ordinary fashion.

After the wedding, we went to live with his parents in Henley Street in Stratford. It was a pleasant enough house, although much smaller than my own home in Shottery. On Henley Street there were two adjoining houses. The front portion of the main house contained the glover's shop, while the front of the second house was leased out, leaving the back part available, and this is where Will and I lodged. A corridor joined the two dwellings, and there was a large garden across the back.

I didn't expect Will's parents to receive me with open arms, and they didn't. His father was civil to me but not cordial, while his mother, who came from a distinguished family and never forgot it, gave me an aloof nod. It wasn't long, though, before they saw that I made Will happy, and that thawed them out.

There's nothing like being married to learn what a person is really like. I soon learned that Will was hasty, impulsive, quick-tempered, and impatient. At the same time, he was kind-hearted and affectionate, and he was endlessly entertaining.

Reading was Will's passion, and he never missed a chance to buy or borrow books whenever he could. Music was another obsession. He organized family concerts, playing the lute or the viol and pressing his younger siblings into learning to play instruments; and everyone sang, Will with his pleasant baritone and I with my alto. And, of course, he still continued to dash off verses on all sorts of topics, including love poems addressed to me.

Will wanted to get out of the glover's shop and into a better occupation, and his chance came through his father's legal problems.

For years John Shakespeare had been involved in buying and selling property all around Stratford, and he often consulted the lawyer, George Camden. Will began sitting in these conferences with his father, and the lawyer was impressed with how quickly Will grasped the issues involved. When Camden's law clerk died, he asked Will if he would like to try his hand at the post, and Will jumped at the chance.

Soon he became fascinated with the law, not merely for his father's cases, but for the whole concept of the English law. He began reading in the law books in Camden's office and talking with the attorney about legal principles. He admired George Camden, who was a stocky man of thirty, with a round face and a genial smile.

"He looks so affable," Will told me, "that opponents can be lulled into ease until his sharp mind pounces on the crucial point and they find themselves outwitted."

Sometimes Will would be irritable for no apparent reason. One day, he burst out with a question that astonished me. We were sitting in our own parlor in the evening. My eyes were on my mending, when I heard Will say, "Anne, put that down and look at me."

I set the garment aside and saw his face sort of twisted, as if he was angry. I simply waited, and he said gruffly, "Do you remember that first time I came to bed with you, at your house in Shottery?"

I smiled. "Of course I remember."

"That wasn't the first time for you, was it?"

I was so startled I couldn't speak.

"You see," he cried, "you can't deny it. You *had* been with someone before me!"

"But, Will, why are you asking me this now?"

His voice shook. "I've always wanted to know. Now I want an answer."

"All right. Yes, I had, when I was very young."

"Is he still around?"

"No, he died at the time of the plague."

"Who was it?"

I said it was Stephen Brent. It took him a minute to remember who that was, and then he said something that almost made me laugh.

"Brent?" he shouted. "But he was married. And he was *old!*"

I glared at him. "He wasn't much older than I am now!"

That infuriated him. He hated being reminded of my age. Then he frowned. "Wait a minute. Wasn't there some story that he harbored a priest and was sent to prison? Is he out now?"

I tried to keep my voice under control. "He died in prison."

"Oh."

He strode around the room for a bit, then came back to me, his voice calmer now. "Did you love him, Anne?"

I wanted to say "No," but I couldn't choke out the word.

"Oh, God, you did!"

Still I said nothing. How could I tell him how desperately I had loved Stephen?

"But you love me now?"

"Of course I do, Will." And I did. So I did what I knew would please him most. I took his arm and we went together up the stairs to our bedroom.

But was that the end of it? Not on your life it wasn't. In the ensuing weeks, Will would keep coming back to the subject of Stephen, seething with jealousy as keen as if it was all happening now, instead of so many years ago. And so it went on. In the end, I flatly refused to answer any questions about Stephen and eventually Will let it drop. Sometimes it seemed to me that Will enjoyed creating crises for the sheer pleasure of having emotional scenes, even though what he felt was genuine enough.

I learned a good deal about Will's parents in those first months of our marriage. Mary Shakespeare was unquestionably a lady, her speech refined and her manner aloof. She was the daughter of Robert Arden of the Warwickshire Ardens, and Will was always pleased that, through his mother, he was a member of a family that traced its ancestry back to the time before William the Conqueror. The family was Catholic, and like many distinguished families, they made outward allegiance to the new church while never really giving up their beliefs, and I soon learned that Mary still secretly had a crucifix and other artifacts in her bedroom, securely hidden.

While Mary's father had left her a considerable fortune in his will, John Shakespeare had made his own way in the world. Son of a tenant farmer, he had come to Stratford as an ambitious youth, learned the glover's trade, prospered, and begun acquiring property in and around Stratford. Friendly and likeable, he had been active in local government, moving up the ladder to the position of Bailiff, the highest office in the town. In that role, he had worn a scarlet gown and presided over official functions, and he had the courtesy title of "Master Shakespeare," giving him the status of a gentleman.

This happy state of affairs went on for a good many years, but Will remembered that the first signs of trouble started when he was about twelve. No longer the Bailiff, but still an alderman, John had stopped going to the meetings of the town council, although attendance was required. His old friend Adrian Quiney and others on the council loyally kept his name on the register for a long time, reluctantly striking him off when others were elected. At the same time, John's financial dealings went sour, and eventually he was borrowing money against Mary's inheritance.

Things went from bad to worse, and Will remembered the quarrels: his mother's protests, and John's angry shouting. John had lost all of the privileges that had gone with his position in the community but was still an amiable fellow among his friends. Sometimes Will would say, "I'll make it all up to my mother some day." However, by the time I arrived on the scene, John and Mary were reconciled and remained a devoted couple.

Meanwhile, as the time drew near for the birth of our child, Will's parents had long since forgotten their first coolness toward me. John had come to admire me, and often said proudly to his friends, "Smart as a whip, that girl. She's a good match for Will!"

Mary was pleased that my speech and manners met with her approval, and she came to be fond of me in her vague way. It seemed to me that Mary often looked at her large family with mild surprise, as if wondering how they had all come to be there. Her old nurse Hetty ran the household, managing the servants and looking after the children. Later, these duties fell to me, while Mary dreamed her way through the years.

Will talked a great deal about the son he expected to have, making plans for him to have the education that he himself had wished for, so when the day came, and after some hours of quite astonishing pain, the child arrived and proved to be a girl, I was afraid Will would be disappointed.

On the contrary, after the child had been washed and wrapped, he gazed at the little creature and took her up into his arms, murmuring, "She's beautiful, Anne." And oddly enough, he was right. Instead of being red and wrinkled, her skin was smooth, and her tiny mouth was like a flower. I had thought she would be named after his mother, but to everyone's surprise Will announced her name would be Susanna. No one in either family had ever been given such an unusual name, but Will chose it for what he called its lovely sound.

He never expressed a word of dismay at not having a son, so enchanted was he with his little Susanna. John Shakespeare snorted that he'd never seen a man so daft over a babe, but Will cared nothing for the opinion of others, always believing his own ways were the best.

Friends often came in of an evening, joining in with our games and our music. Being part of a warm and lively household was a new experience for me, and I liked it. John's old friend, Adrian Quiney, was a regular, practically a member of the family because of his loyalty to John in his time of troubles. His wife had died, and his son Richard, who had been at school with Will, often came with his young wife.

And that's how I first met Richard Quiney. I didn't like him from the first, but I never thought he would end up being murdered. With his head of thick auburn hair that fell in soft waves over his forehead, Richard was an extremely handsome young man, and no one was more aware of it than Richard himself. He expected all women to succumb to his charms, and unfortunately many of them did. His young wife adored him, and if he dallied elsewhere, as rumor had it, she made no protest.

What I hated most about Richard was his patronizing attitude toward Will. He would often remark on Will's intellectual superiority. "Always top of the class," he would say, "while I was still struggling with my Latin." And his smug smile implied that he was perfectly content not to be such a drudge. Richard was tall and strongly built, while Will was slender and of average height, and Richard had an infuriating habit of jovially clapping Will on the shoulder, as if they were great pals.

"How do you put up with him?" I would mutter to Will, and he would laugh. "It's been like that all my life. You know that anyone with the name of Quiney is sacred in this family. Richard's tiresome, but what can I do?" And I saw his point. Both Mary and John adored Richard.

Richard's wife was expecting their first child soon after our Susanna was born, and she told me she was hoping for a boy because that would please Richard, but she couldn't help longing for a little girl like mine. I saw her happily preparing for the new baby, feeling well and not anticipating any trouble. Yet tragedy struck with no warning. The baby was healthy, but the doctor could not stop her bleeding, and within hours she was dead.

We were all profoundly shocked, and Richard seemed at first to be devastated, but it wasn't long before he was back to normal again. If I had thought he would devote himself to his little son, I couldn't have been more wrong. His wife's parents came, and evidently with Richard's willing consent, took little Tom back to their home in the far north, near a big lake called Windermere.

At first we inquired about the child, but Richard would always say it was too painful for him to speak of it. A likely story, I thought. It was obvious to me that he simply didn't care. I noticed he made no effort to visit little Tom nor to have the child come to live with him.

About the time of our daughter's first birthday, Will had begun to grow restless and to talk again about his early yearning for going to live in London. "I might go into the printer's trade," he would say, "or I could be a law clerk there." He ignored the fact that we would have nowhere to live and that everyone knew it cost more to live in the city.

I also noticed that he was growing bored with his legal work. It had become a routine and his position as clerk didn't offer the mental challenge he would have liked.

Then I discovered I was with child again, and at first Will was excited at the prospect of having another infant to dote on. I think it gradually occurred to him that with another child, the dream of going to London was pretty remote, for I heard no more about it.

From time to time a company of players would come to Stratford on their tour of the provinces, and we all went to the performances. Will sneered when the play was weak or poorly written, and he always assessed the skill of the actors. He would remember lines from the play, reciting them and saying, "This is how it ought to be done!" The play he liked best was written by a young man named Christopher Marlowe, and Will was awestruck. "That man is a great poet," he would say. "He is head and shoulders above all the others."

In this pregnancy, I had become extremely large, causing predictions that this time it would be a boy. And indeed it was, but when shouts of joy greeted his arrival, the midwife announced that there was a second child, and a girl was born. Will was delighted with the boy but showed equal pleasure in the little girl. The Sadlers, friends of the Shakespeare family, were chosen as godparents, and their names—Hamnet and Judith—were given to the twins at their christening.

That was in the month of February, and things went along for another year or so.

It was in the spring of the following year, when Susanna was three and the twins toddling, that the event occurred that changed all of our lives forever. The troupe of players known as the Earl of Leicester's Men came to Stratford and gave a performance that Will considered to be the finest he had ever seen. The principal actor, James Burbage, struck Will as an actor of such talent that it bordered on genius. "If I could do that, Anne," he said to me, "it would be more satisfying than anything I can imagine."

The very day after the performance we had attended, Will wasted no time. He went to the inn where the company was lodged and talked with one of the players whose performance he had admired. That evening, he told me what he had learned. There were different levels for the actors. At the top were the actors who were members of the company and shared in the profits. Then there were actors who were not "shareholders." Below these were the "hired men," who might be taken on for a short time, if they were needed for particular parts, or who sometimes remained on a permanent basis. Finally, there were the boy apprentices, who were paid little but had a sure future if they were successful.

"Why all the questions, Will?" I asked. But I already knew what was coming. And indeed, the following morning, Will went back to the inn and asked Mr. Burbage how he might go about becoming an actor.

"He gave me a sharp look," Will told me. "Then he told me that two of his players had died recently in the plague, one of them his chief musician, and he asked if I were skilled in music. I played the viol for him and sang, and then he asked me to read some lines."

Evidently Mr. Burbage liked what he heard, and that's how it came about. Will was to be taken on trial as a "hired man." No promises were made. He would accompany the players on their current tour, and when they returned to London, a decision would be reached.

I was stunned. "Do you mean you intend to leave us and go to London?"

Will put his arms around me and looked lovingly into my eyes. "Do you really want me to turn down this great chance, Anne?"

What could I say? I wondered how long his enthusiasm would last, but at least he would be doing something that challenged him, and I supposed that was better than sulking around Stratford.

So Will secured a leave of absence from George Camden's law office and went cheerfully off to his new life as an actor on the stage.

I wasn't happy about it, but I didn't see that I had much choice. When Will wanted something badly enough, he was likely to get it.

iv

It was the month of September before we heard from Will. The big news was that when the company had finished the tour and come back to London, Mr. Burbage had engaged Will for the current season. He had been put in charge of the musicians, and was working hard at learning his craft as an actor.

When George Camden told us that Will had resigned from his clerkship, John Shakespeare said he didn't understand it all, and Camden said, with his genial smile, "I always thought young Will would make a name for himself some day, but I never expected he would go off to be an actor!"

For a fellow who loved to write poems, Will wasn't much of a letter writer. We heard a few bits of news, but nothing much until he announced he was coming home in the month of August for a visit. Poor Mary looked tearful when she heard this. "A visit? Then he will be going back?"

But I wasn't surprised. I was sure Will would go back as long as he was wanted. And when he arrived, there could be no doubt. He loved what he was doing. He talked endlessly about the life in the theater and the challenge of becoming a really fine actor. He admired the well-written plays and was pleased that the men in his company were disciplined professionals. We heard about the problems facing all the acting companies. The Puritans hated the theaters and were always trying to shut them down. Fortunately, Queen Elizabeth herself loved the drama and liked to please her subjects in matters like this, so popular demand usually prevailed to get the theaters open again.

I had wondered if after the excitement of his life in London, Will would be bored with tame old Stratford, but not so. For a month, he clearly reveled in being at home with family and friends. He spent hours with the children. Susanna, now five, was his adored first-born. The twins, age three, tumbled and shrieked, climbing over their papa like puppies, and Will enjoyed it all. I'll say this for Will that, whatever his shortcomings, he was always a devoted father. But by the end of the month, he grew restless and irritable. He had the children in tears, and, except when we were in bed, he snapped at me whatever I said or did. I can't say I was sorry when it came time for him to leave.

Chapter 2

POET AND PLAYWRIGHT

i

During the following year, we heard some astonishing news from Will. In addition to his acting, he had written a play, and it had been produced! When he came home, he told us how it all came about. It started when he came across a play about a Roman emperor named Titus Andronicus. He thought the play was poorly written but saw that the plot, full of vengeance, bloody sacrifices, and other acts of violence, was just the sort of thing popular audiences loved. In the end, he had completely rewritten the original, in verse that was much admired. Shortly before he came home to Stratford, the play had been performed by his own company and then at the rival Rose Theater, where it made almost as much money as Christopher Marlowe's *Tamburlaine*. This thrilled him, because he admired young Marlowe's work above all others.

During the next few years, this was the pattern of our lives. Will came home for a month or so whenever he had permission, and that was no easy trip. It took three or four days of miserable travel, always in danger from robbers, and using whatever horses could be found for hire along the way. He brought working copies of his new plays for me to read, and he was always writing another one during his time at home. He wrote plays on the lives of English kings, he wrote comedies, he wrote whatever his company needed at the time, and the audiences loved them all. His income increased every year, and he was happy as a lark.

This was all very well for Will, but what sort of life was it for me?

I can't say I liked having an absentee husband, but I got used to it, and it could have been worse. I had a comfortable home and healthy children, which was far more than many had, and I told myself to make the best of it.

Then one day a welcome change came into our lives.

The children came running into the house to tell me there were a boy and girl near their own age on the other side of our garden hedge.

Susanna's eyes were glowing. "The girl's name is Agnes and she is the same age as me!"

Judith chimed. "And there's a boy named David—"

And Hamnet echoed. "He's just my size. Come and see!"

I followed the three of them out to the low hedge that ran between our garden and that of the house that faced on the lane beyond, and there stood a lovely, dark-haired young woman. "I'm Rosanna Wilson," she said, holding out her hand.

Dear, sweet Rosanna. If I ever felt fed up with Will going off to London and leaving me in Stratford to cope, I had only to compare my lot to Rosanna's to put a stop to any self-pity. As we became friends, I learned that it had been two years since her husband, a young officer in the Queen's Navy, had been killed in an engagement with the Spanish. She had stayed on in London for a time, in the home of the Wilsons, her husband's people, but that didn't last. His mother was no longer living and her father-in-law had remarried, to a woman who didn't welcome Rosanna and her two little ones into her household. So Rosanna had now come back to her native Warwickshire.

"I've been living at the Hall since I came back," she said, "but it's rather isolated there, and it's better for the children to be here in the town."

Larch Hall was the ancestral home of the wealthy Bushell family several miles outside of Stratford, where she had grown up. Her father had died when she was seven, and her mother followed only a year later. Now she had no family left except for her bachelor brother Edward and a cousin who lived in Italy in a town called Siena.

Rosanna clearly adored her brother. "Edward has been so kind," she said, with her gentle smile. "He owns many properties all around the county, and he has given me this lovely house so that we can be here in Stratford."

It was indeed a fine house, with plenty of room for servants, and Rosanna soon settled in. Our children were wonderfully matched in age. Susanna and Agnes were both seven, while her David and my twins had all turned five. We soon had a gate installed in the hedge between our gardens for easy access and were constantly together.

Will's mother welcomed Rosanna as a fellow member of the gentry. "I was an Arden, my dear," Mary said, "and of course we knew the Bushells, although my home at Wilmcote was many miles from your Larch Hall."

As for John, he beamed at our pretty new neighbor. "I've met your brother through property deals. A fine young man is Edward Bushell."

Soon Rosanna and her brother were included in our Saturday evening gatherings. As I saw more of Edward, I noticed that he seemed to spend a lot of his time hanging about on the fringes of titled circles. His conversation was sprinkled with anecdotes about the aristocratic persons he claimed as his dearest friends. Their cousin Carla was married to an Italian nobleman, and Edward always referred to her as "the Contessa." I may have been secretly amused at Edward, but he was good to his sister and that was enough for me.

The first time Rosanna and Edward came to one of our evening parties, she sat shyly in a corner. All the regulars were there around John and Mary's fireside, including Adrian Quiney and other old buddies of that generation. Our good friend George Camden, the lawyer, was there. And, needless to say, handsome Richard Quiney was the life of the party, tossing his reddish locks and oozing charm.

Rosanna sat in her corner quietly smiling, but it wasn't until the music started that we could coax her into joining.

Mary said, "You have a lovely voice, my dear."

Edward Bushell smiled proudly. "Our mother sang, and my sister has her voice."

After another song or two, the conversation became lively, as usual, and Rosanna retreated again to her corner. John told an amusing story about the farmer who had recently sued him on a false claim and how George Camden had defended him.

George laughed. "The fellow put a value on an old horse that could barely hobble and tried to pass off another animal in its place. It didn't take much legal skill to settle that one."

Presently, I saw Richard move to a chair next to Rosanna, and I thought, "Here we go." Ignoring the general chatter, Richard was speaking softly to her, and Rosanna looked at him with her lovely dark eyes, smiling with much the same maternal expression she bestowed on her children. She seemed to have no notion that he was flirting with her, and Richard, looking baffled, finally moved away.

Rosanna was delighted with the evening, and her response was much the same as mine had been soon after my marriage. "I've never been part of a family that had such good times together," she said to me. "I was often lonely, growing up at the Hall. Edward is five years older than I, and of course much of the time he was away at school or off with his friends."

She often said to me, "What would I do without you, Anne?" And I felt the same.

When our little boys turned six, it was time for Hamnet and David to go to the primary school. It was a painful shock for Judith when Hamnet went off each day. The twins had been inseparable all their short lives, and in the afternoons she would rush down the road to meet the boys, hanging on Hamnet's arm as they walked home.

Rosanna and I shared the duties of giving lessons to the little girls, as of course there was no school for them. Susanna and Agnes, both aged eight, were bright and studious, while little Judith was equally bright, but mischievous and less attentive.

One day Rosanna said, "It's good being able to give the lessons ourselves, Anne. After my mother died, I had governesses, and some were kind and some were not." Her eyes misted, and I thought that even though my parents and my brother had never shown me much affection, at least they had been there. I hadn't been rattling about that big house with servants who cared even less.

Rosanna was impressed with how much I loved to read. "I always did read whatever my teachers assigned," she said, "but I never cared much for my lessons, except when the music master came, and now I seldom read much. But you read all the time, Anne. And you *know* so much about things I never even heard of. You can teach the children far more than I can!"

I knew what she was thinking—how was it that although I had never had her advantages, yet I seemed to be far beyond her in knowledge?

Remembering my childhood, I said quietly, "I don't know why it was, but from the moment I made my brother show me his primer, I was mad to learn, and once you can read simple things, you can go on from there on your own. But remember, Rosanna, that you can teach the children French and Italian when they are ready. Even the boys won't get that at school. It will soon be all Latin and Greek for them."

I knew that she grieved painfully for her young husband, but she never complained. She even offered sympathy to me. "I know how you miss Will when he is away," she would say in her gentle voice. I wasn't about to grumble about Will after that.

In addition to Rosanna, I had also found a good friend in George Camden, someone I could consult when I needed help or advice. More important, George was enormously impressed with the quality of Will's plays. Since I always made copies of the plays Will had brought with him, and of those he wrote while he was at home, George eagerly read them and we spent hours going over each one.

ii

Thus my life went along pleasantly enough. It may not have been as exciting as Will's, but I was content.

One day, a year or so later, when Will had gone back to

London after a month at home, I noticed that Richard kept turning up at my side. If I went for a walk along the Avon to watch the swans, there he was, remarking on the lovely weather and walking along beside me. If I went into a shop, there he was as I came out, ready to tag along.

Thursday was market day in Stratford, when people from all over the area came in to do their shopping. The stalls were set up in the square, and every merchant in town put out his best offerings, while farmers brought in their butter and eggs and fresh produce. I wasn't surprised to see Richard picking up a few items and then coming over to me, offering to help carry my purchases back to the house. I did have several full bags, and the help was welcome, but I asked myself, what on earth does he want?

I got the answer to that soon enough. When he had put the bags down, he made no move to leave. The children were at Rosanna's place and we were alone. I said, "Thank you, Richard," and moved toward the door, but he stopped me, standing close to me and looking into my eyes.

"I want to talk to you, Anne. You know you are still a beautiful woman. When I was a schoolboy, I used to see you come into town and I would dream about you at night. Sometimes I can't believe that good old Will was the one to carry you off."

I said nothing. If he had expected any encouragement, he didn't get it, but that didn't stop Richard. He was perfectly aware that I had never been dazzled by him, and I suppose he regarded me as a challenge.

His voice was soft and caressing. "I know Will is a brainy chap, Anne, but there's more to life than that. When he's away in London, you must get pretty lonely here."

He was right, I did. When he pulled me to him and held me in a passionate kiss, I felt his body against mine and thought for one brief moment how tempting it would be to engage in that sexual pleasure I was denied for such long months at a time. But that feeling was gone in a flash.

I gave him a push. "Come off it, Richard. You know I love Will. Don't be stupid!"

The truth is, I wanted to smack him, but it wouldn't have done to insult a Quiney in that household. He swaggered off, muttering that I was a fool to turn him down. I was pretty sure he wouldn't try it again, and I said nothing to anyone, not even to Rosanna, and certainly not to Will.

Around that time, rumors began to fly about Richard being in debt. The Quineys had always been a prosperous family. Old Adrian not only had a thriving business as a wool draper, he also bought and sold property, as John Shakespeare did. Now Richard was involved in similar investments. He had become great friends with Rosanna's brother Edward, and the two of them were often together at Larch Hall where Edward lived, or going off to London on various business enterprises. Richard obviously benefited from having a wealthy friend, and Edward seemed to be under the spell of Quiney's charm.

Then one day, we learned that Richard had brought home an attractive lady he had met in London, who was living with him as his "housekeeper," though I doubted if she did much around the house. Good luck to her, I thought. I hope she keeps him occupied. I ought to have known, though, that Richard Quiney was one of those bad pennies that would always turn up to plague our lives.

One day in the spring of that year, I had just stepped out of the front door when George Camden came by in his pony cart.

"Anne," he called out, "I'm going over toward Evesham. Want to come along?"

I smiled. "Yes, indeed. I'm ready for a break!"

The children were with Rosanna, and I stepped inside to tell the servant to let Mistress Wilson know that I would be gone till suppertime. I took a warm cloak off the hook, and went out to join George in the cart.

It was one of those magic days when the sun turned the recent raindrops into diamonds and gave out enough warmth to make people believe that summer might really come some day.

As we jogged along, George got onto the subject of clients and their behavior patterns.

"Some are sensible and listen to my legal advice on how to manage their affairs. Sometimes I get one who tells me in no uncertain terms what she wants and what she doesn't want. I had one of those recently who refused to allow one of her sons to receive the inheritance his father had left him in his will.

" 'It must all go to the other boy,' " she said, with her lips tightly pressed and a voice like a bullhorn. " 'He's the one as never gave trouble. But the older one don't deserve a shilling. He'll waste it all in no time. So I expect you to fix that, Master Camden.' "

George laughed. "She would not listen to reason. She treated me with what I took to be her habitual manner with the now-deceased husband, poor chap."

"What did you do?"

"I decided to leave it to the judge in probate to set her straight."

"And did that convince her?"

He grinned. "Not on your life. She still blames me and is convinced I could have done what she wanted. That's one of the joys of law practice. I think Will is better off in his theater!"

I laughed. "But not all clients are like that, surely?"

"No, indeed. The one we are visiting today is quite the opposite, and more typical, I must say. Her husband, Thomas Fletcher, was a client of mine for many years and was as fine a fellow as ever you'd meet, and Rebecca is a sweet little woman who wouldn't say boo to a goose. They have a fine house and a good property, as you'll see, and she wants to sell it and come into Stratford to live with her daughter, who is an invalid with a young daughter. Rebecca tells me she has an offer on the property and wants my advice."

After an hour or so, we left the main road and went along a tree-lined lane, through a tiny village, and up a hill, where we drew up in front of a fine house that reminded me of my old home in Shottery.

We were welcomed by the widow, George introducing me and indicating that he had brought me along to give him a woman's opinion of the house. Rebecca nodded and said she knew John Shakespeare's glover's shop in Stratford but seemed to know nothing of Will.

Beaming at me, she said, "Let us have some refreshment first, and then I can show you about."

After a sumptuous feast of delicious little cakes that had obviously been prepared for the visit, George lit his pipe and waited while Rebecca proudly took me on a tour of her well-kept house, speaking shyly of her dear husband and how much he had relied upon Master Camden for advice and help in all matters of concern.

Back downstairs, I gave George a glowing report of the excellent condition of the house, supporting his excuse for my being there. He nodded solemnly, thanked me, and turned to Rebecca.

"Now, you say you have received an offer for the property?"

"Yes! A young man from Stratford named Richard Quiney came the other day and offered the sum of three hundred pounds. I said I would have to consult with Nate—that's Thomas's brother—and with you, Master Camden, but Master Quiney said he was sure I couldn't do better, and he insisted I take fifty pounds to start."

George and I exchanged a glance. Why the big hurry? And where did Richard get the money? He must have something up his sleeve.

George asked calmly, "Did you sign anything, Rebecca?"

Her face flushed. "Well, just a little piece of paper, almost a scrap. He said it was just a receipt for the money. He is such a charming young man. I'm sure he is reliable."

Of course he is, I thought wryly.

There was a sudden loud banging on the outer door, and we looked up to see a heavily-built man with graying hair brush past the servant and stop short as he saw the three of us in the parlor.

Rebecca seemed to shrink back in her chair, and her voice quavered. "Oh, Nate! I'm—that is—I didn't expect you, but I am glad you are here."

She looked anything but glad to me, but she bravely went on. "Nate, you know Master Camden, of course. And this is Missus Shakespeare, from Stratford."

Nate Fletcher sat down on a chair that creaked under his weight.

"Hello, Camden," he said, in a resounding voice, with a nod in George's direction. Then his eyes moved toward me, and he took his time studying me.

"Missus Shakespeare, eh? Is your husband the actor fellow that's on the boards in London?"

His tone was more like a sneer than a question, and I stared into his face and said nothing.

George spoke quietly. "William Shakespeare is a distinguished member of the Earl of Leicester's company in London, yes. Now, Nate, we are talking with Rebecca about—"

Nate's voice rose to a new level and he turned his gaze on his sister-in-law. "Yes, Rebecca, what's this I hear about you taking an offer on this place without consulting me first?"

Poor Rebecca quailed. "I meant to ask you, Nate, but—"

"I should think so. I'm Tom's brother, and you can rely on me now to look after things for you."

Rebecca's eyes brimmed over and she groped for the handkerchief in her pocket. "Tom always told me to see Master Camden if I needed help."

"Oh, he did, did he? Well, I think a member of your own family might have something to say about that."

George cleared his throat. "Actually, Nate, although Rebecca may certainly consult you if she wishes, she is not obliged to do so. According to Thomas's will, which I am familiar with, as I drew it for him, the decision over the sale of the property is left to Rebecca."

Nate growled. "Never mind that. She might ask me first."

Timidly, Rebecca gave him a conciliatory little smile. "But Nate, Master Quiney gave me fifty pounds to start."

"Oh, he did, did he?" The scowl subsided into a grunt. "Well, how much did he offer?"

George answered. "Three hundred pounds, I understand. Sound fair to you, Nate?"

Another grunt, but a grudging nod. "Could be, could be."

We took our leave, with thanks from Rebecca and no further growls from Nate Fletcher.

On the ride back to Stratford, George confirmed what I had suspected. "When I drew up Tom Fletcher's will a few years ago, he specifically told me to fix it so that his brother Nate would have no control over the property. He said Nate had his own holdings but was always greedy for more, and Tom knew that his brother would bully Rebecca if he could."

I said, "At least, he seemed to think the three hundred was a fair price, so it may all work out well in the end."

George grinned. "Let's hope so."

We should have known that anything that involved Richard Quiney would always be trouble. It was no more than a week later when I was at Rosanna's place doing our lessons with the girls when we heard loud voices and went to the front window in time to see George Camden and Nate Fletcher standing in the lane face to face, in a violent argument. Like most houses in the town, there was little space between the front of the house and the lane, and through the open window we could hear Nate shouting, "Why should Rebecca have to give the money back?"

George shouted, "What are you talking about, Nate?"

Nate raised his fist. "Look here, Camden. Quiney wants to back out of the deal, and he wants his fifty pounds back."

His voice lowered to a more normal tone, George asked, "What does Rebecca say?"

"You know Rebecca. She says maybe she ought to give it back."

"So what's the big problem? Why do you care if she does?"

"Well, she hasn't got it right now."

"What do you mean, she hasn't got it?"

We could see Nate's face flushing to a deep red. "Well, I borrowed it from her to settle some expenses, but I'll give it back as soon as I can."

"All right. So Quiney will have to wait."

"But he says he wants it now, and Rebecca says it's her legal obligation to give it to him."

"Where did she get that idea?"

Now Nate's voice rose to a shout again. "You ought to know the answer to that, Camden. Quiney told her that's what *you* said, that it was her legal obligation."

George shouted back. "I did no such thing! Have you been drinking, Nate?"

"So what if I have? You're just like all the lawyers. You'll lie about anything if you have to."

George said, "You'd better calm down."

But this seemed to inflame Nate, whose anger rose till he lost all control. His clenched fist, with the strength of his heavy body behind it, struck George and knocked him to the ground. Rosanna and I ran to the door and out into the lane, bending over George, and when I looked up, I saw the back of Nate Fletcher disappearing around the corner.

Rosanna's menservants brought George into her parlor, where we soon had him stretched on a sofa and covered with a shawl. When we had sent for the doctor, Rosanna brought a cloth soaked in warm water and gently removed the blood from the wound on George's face, murmuring soothing words, as she would to a child.

The doctor, when he came, found bruises but no broken bones, saying, "Well, Master Camden, who did this to you?"

George gave Rosanna and me a warning glance.

"Don't know," he said to the doctor.

The doctor looked at us and we shook our heads. With a wry smile that said, "A likely story," he picked up his bag. "Well, keep him warm and give him some brandy." And he hurried off.

An hour later, George insisted he was fully recovered, and with many thanks to Rosanna and over our protests, he walked back to his own home.

The next day, I sent a note to George asking him to return a book, a message which he fully understood.

"All right, Anne," he grinned, when he turned up at my door with the book in question. "I know what you want to know."

I put him in a chair, gave us each a brandy, and said the obvious. "Why did you say you didn't know who attacked you?"

"The last thing I want is to publicize the whole affair. It's pretty humiliating to be knocked down in a public place, and it doesn't add to the dignity of my profession. The fact is, Nate came to me this morning, full of apology and terrified I would have him up for assault. I let him stew for a bit, and then assured him that if he didn't talk about it, I wouldn't either. Now, of course, he is furious with Richard. He saw him last night and Richard insisted he had only told Rebecca that he *thought* I had said she had to return the money."

I said, "So far as I'm concerned, Nate can knock Richard down any time. He deserves it. I wonder where he got the fifty pounds and how he expected to get the rest."

"He's been hitting everybody he knows for a loan, as usual. He had already tried me, but I refused."

"Doesn't his father usually pay up for him?"

"I'm afraid so. But I think Adrian has finally cut him off."

"What about Edward? Won't he help out his dear friend?"

"He probably would, but he's off to Italy visiting his cousin the Contessa, and Richard wants the money now."

"Any dealings with Richard are bad news," I said.

"Yes, I'm afraid so. Well, I must be going." Then there was a pause, and he said softly, "Rosanna was very kind yesterday."

I looked at George's round, pleasant face. Not handsome, but what was perhaps better, a man of fine character and keen mind. Why had he never married again, after the loss of his young wife? No one knew, and in spite of our enduring friendship, I never asked.

I was amused when within a month, the whole crisis between Richard and Nate Fletcher had been solved, and the two mortal enemies were fast friends. John Shakespeare, hearing the story from Richard, had gone out to look at Rebecca's property and decided to buy it himself, hoping to sell it later at a profit. Richard was now off the hook and Nate Fletcher was satisfied. John's dealings had been prospering for some time, and the family fortunes were once again in stable condition.

That was all very well, but I was truly startled when who should turn up at a fireside evening but Nate Fletcher. John, knowing nothing of Nate's attack on George, had said to him, "Nate's really a good sort, you know. A bit rough, perhaps, but I like the fellow!"

John liked just about everybody, and no one ever objected. Fortunately, Nate lived too far out to be a frequent visitor, but when he did come into town, he would see Rebecca, who now lived with her daughter, as she had wished. The daughter had had a terrible fall and was confined to an invalid chair, and Rebecca was much needed.

One day I met Rebecca in the high street, walking with her granddaughter, a remarkably pretty girl.

"Libby is seventeen now," Rebecca said proudly. "She has just started helping at your family's glover's shop, now that I am here to help with my daughter."

I smiled at the girl. "And do you like being in the shop, my dear?"

Lovely dark eyes looked into mine, warm but serious.

"Oh, yes, ma'am. Very much."

"I shall look in on you soon," I promised, and went on with my errands.

Since my marriage, I had rarely gone into the shop. When Will had taken the post as clerk to George Camden, his younger brother had taken charge of the shop, and, unlike Will, was glad of the chance. He had proved to be an excellent manager, and John was pleased.

Now, when I stepped in to chat with Libby, I was told that she was doing very well, had learned quickly, and was much liked by the customers, which was no surprise.

"It was Uncle Nate who got this place for me," she told me solemnly. "He is so good to me."

Now I noticed that when Nate came in the evening, he talked a great deal about his grandniece. He had never married, and it looked as if any paternal feelings he had were lavished on his "little Libby."

When I told him I thought she was a very pretty girl, he beamed with pleasure. "She is that. And just as good as can be. She's never given a mite of trouble, has our Libby."

George was there and we exchanged glances, agreeing later that human nature was full of surprises.

I said, "Who would guess that loud-mouthed, hot-tempered Nate Fletcher was capable of tender affection?"

George laughed. "I thought I'd seen it all, but there's always another one."

iii

That was the year when a visitation of the plague in London was so severe that the theaters were closed by decree for several months, and I expected that at last Will would come home for a long stay. So I was astonished when Will wrote that he wouldn't be coming to Stratford, as he had been invited to spend some weeks at Titchfield in Hampshire, the country house of the Earl of Southampton.

I'll come home later on, Anne, he wrote. *The Earl may be an important patron, and I must take advantage of this opportunity.*

Well, all right, I thought, an aristocratic patron was a good prospect. On his last visit Will had mentioned the young Earl, who often came to the theater with a group of friends and chatted with the players. Will described him as a beautiful young man, with fine eyes and golden hair that fell to his collar in waves and ringlets. Witty and charming, he was evidently adored equally by both the men and the ladies in his coterie. He sounded a bit foppish to me, but if he could further Will's career, that was fine.

Christmas passed, and some time in February Will wrote that the Earl and his party had come back to London. "I am back in my lodgings, working very hard on a long poem that I plan to dedicate to the Earl, and I must stay here till it is finished."

I was furious. So why couldn't he just as well write his poem at home in Stratford instead of in London? The plague was still raging there. Wouldn't he be better off away from there?

I was about to write a heated reply along those lines, but then I sat down and thought about it. I was really surprised that Will had had the chance to come home and hadn't taken it. In spite of his growing success, as both actor and writer, he had always seemed to me to be rooted in Stratford. His work was in London, but his true life was at home. Or so I had thought.

Was all that changing? Or was I beginning to worry over

nothing? I had never gone in for the role of the nagging wife, and it didn't seem the right time to start now, so I decided to wait and see.

Rosanna and I were busy with the children, and some amusement came into our lives when her cousin from Italy came for a visit. Edward Bushell made the introduction in his formal manner. "May I present Carla Bandini, Contessa di Lucca?"

If he thought I was going to curtsey or be awestruck, he was disappointed. I simply held out my hand to her and said we were all happy she had come to Stratford. I saw at once her resemblance to Rosanna. After all, their mothers had been sisters. Both were pretty women, but while Rosanna was not vain of her appearance, Carla thought of little else.

We were together almost daily during her visit, and her conversation was filled with talk of the latest fashions in gowns and of the jewels her husband gave her. Susanna and Agnes giggled when she did their hair up like fine ladies, and Hamnet and David grinned when she told them what handsome young gentlemen they were, while Judith looked on with shining eyes.

Carla adored the popular pastime of astrology and attributed every incident to the action of the stars. She made notes of all our birthdays and made ominous predictions according to the sign of the Zodiac under which each of us was born. She was also given to seeing visions of people long dead.

The children were spellbound as she spoke one day. "There is a turret at our palazzo in Siena, and one dark night, when I climbed up the winding stairs, I saw my grandmother. She was standing against the stone wall, wearing a long white shroud, with her gray hair hanging below her shoulders. She didn't speak, but she held out her arms toward me."

Little David whispered, "And then what did she do, Aunt Carla?"

Carla's dark eyes glowed. "She moved backward into the wall, and as I watched, she passed through the stones and disappeared!"

There were similar tales of the disembodied appearances of titled gentlemen who had been her admirers before their untimely deaths.

Carla seemed to me to be scatter-brained and silly, but I kept that opinion from Rosanna, who listened devotedly to all her cousin's chatter. She needed to cling to the only female relation she had, and I was happy to see that Carla seemed genuinely fond of her cousin.

Then Carla's husband arrived, and she seemed more subdued. I noticed she often looked at him before speaking, as if she feared his disapproval. This was all the more surprising, as he seemed absolutely devoted to her. The Count was twenty years her senior, but a handsome man, distinguished and courtly in manner. At our social evenings, everyone admired him. Mary and John were entranced with both Carla and her husband, and Richard Quiney, who turned up shortly before they went back to Italy, put himself out to be especially pleasant to both of them. Good thing the Count was here, I thought, or Richard would certainly have tried his luck with beautiful Carla.

iv

In the end, it was the month of May before Will came home, and I still hadn't decided what to say about his long absence. Would he be restless and anxious to get back to

London? I tried not to think about it, but it wasn't easy. What excuse would he give?

He arrived in great spirits, saying how glad he was to be home again. When his mother remarked tearfully that he had been gone a dreadfully long time, he said, all smiles, that he supposed he had, but here he was now.

He was bursting with the news that his long poem, *Venus and Adonis*, had been published, and he proudly showed us the beautiful little volume, with its dedication to "Henry Wriothesley, Earl of Southampton."

John looked curiously at the Earl's surname. "What kind of a name is that?"

Will laughed. "I know it looks odd, Dad, but it's pronounced 'Risley.' "

John and Mary were delighted with Will's accomplishments. When he described to us his visits to the Earl's country house and to his palatial home in London, John was impressed. "An Earl, eh? You're moving in some exalted circles, I'd say."

Mary merely looked at Will with her complacent little smile. "But it's not surprising. After all, my dear, you *are* an Arden."

I was sure that his parents saw Will as much the same as usual, but what I saw in Will was a transformation. Those weeks at the house party at Titchfield had plunged him into a life that had dazzled him with its sophistication. Titled lords and ladies mingled freely with artists, poets, and musicians, engaging in bantering conversations and exchanging barbs of wit. It was a game in which only the clever could survive, and I could see that Will had reveled in his ability to hold his own in this rarefied company. It was not so much the wealth or the titles that impressed him. What he loved was his participation in a life where wit and intellect were exercised and prized above all else.

So it was that I had held my tongue and said nothing about his prolonged stay in London. He seemed glad enough to be home again, and I thought, why not let well enough alone?

We were sitting in the garden one day soon after his arrival, when I asked Will to tell me more about the Earl of Southampton. He began in rather a dry tone. "He became the Earl when he was only eight years of age and became a royal ward of William Cecil, Lord Burghley. He's the Queen's most powerful minister, as everyone knows. At the age of fifteen, the Earl was sent to St. John's College, Cambridge, and then to the law school in London at the Grays Inn."

I didn't quite yawn, but I waited for something more personal, and I wasn't disappointed. Will became more animated as he went on.

"When the Earl was seventeen, Burghley determined that his ward should marry Burghley's granddaughter, Lady Elizabeth Vere. The poor boy was horrified. He told me himself that he was too young to marry, even if the lady had been a beauty, which she was not, and he simply defied his guardian and refused. Why, even now, Anne, the lad has only a faint line of hair on his lip, and he is nineteen years of age. At seventeen, he was truly a child. He had no experience of life."

I repressed a smile. "And has he more experience now?"

Will nodded. "Quite a lot, I should say. You see, everyone is in love with him."

As the days went by, the young man became part of every conversation. If food was mentioned, we heard a clever remark the Earl had made concerning the roast lamb. If horses were mentioned, we heard the Earl's witty discourse upon riding. Because of Will's skill at mimicry, he would adopt what was clearly the Earl's voice and manner when quoting these priceless gems of wit, so that I felt him as a living presence and could sense the allure of his charm.

I could see that it was no coincidence that Will, to please his patron, had chosen this story of Venus and Adonis from his old favorite, Ovid, with its passionate portrayal of the beauty of the young Adonis. Now I learned that during those months in London, while he was writing his poem, Will had been often at Southampton House. The Earl and his circle adored erotic love stories about mythological figures, and they were all mad about Will's *Venus*, making him the celebrity of the moment.

I could understand their enthusiasm. The poetry was gloriously lush. I read through it with astonishment and delight. Will often read passages aloud to all of us, the children understanding little, but mesmerized by his voice as he read. I was amused to see that when his mother was present, he omitted lines that he thought might shock her, such as Venus saying to the beautiful young Adonis:

I'll be a park, and thou shalt be my deer,
Feed where you wilt, on mountain or in dale;
Graze on my lips; and if those hills be dry,
Stray lower, where the pleasant fountains lie.

Will announced with modest pride that the Earl had presented him with a generous sum of money. That's all very well, I thought, but there is real passion in all those lines about the beautiful Adonis. This wasn't written just for money. Look at those moving lines when the boy goes hunting and is killed by the boar, and Venus laments:

Alas, poor world, what treasure hast thou lost!
What face remains alive that's worth the viewing?
Whose tongue is music now . . . ?
The flowers are sweet, their colours fresh and trim;
But true-sweet beauty lived and died with him.

Will was certainly enamored. Was this another of his enthusiasms that wouldn't last? Time would tell.

The death of young Adonis was a reminder of a real tragedy that had occurred shortly before Will left London. In the month of May, the young playwright, Christopher Marlowe, had been killed by some companions in a tavern brawl. Although Marlowe had been a rival, Will felt nothing but sorrow at his loss. "He was my age," Will said, "and look what he accomplished. Will I ever match him?"

After all that dazzling life among the rich and titled, I expected that Will would soon grow restless in tame old Stratford, but instead, he plunged into writing a new play and during the day was intensely absorbed in the work. In the evenings he basked in the lively gatherings of friends and family, and seemed to be content.

One evening when everyone had gone, I stood alone at the window for a moment, thinking that it had been ten years since Will and I were married. Did I have regrets? Plenty of times when he was gone for months, I would resent being left alone. Now I wondered if he had other women in his life. What about all those dazzling ladies in the Earl of Southampton's circle? Was I just a dull housewife to him by now? Oh, well, no use borrowing trouble, as my mother used to say. When we were in bed, he was as passionate as ever, so why worry?

I had told Will the story of Richard Quiney and Nate Fletcher, and how they had become friends again after

Nate's quarrel with George, and Will had laughed. "Richard always seems to get by with it, whatever escapade he's entangled in."

Then one day, I saw Richard Quiney go into our glover's shop, looking at the samples spread out along the counter, and I followed him in.

"Buying gloves, Richard?" I asked.

He looked slightly uncomfortable. "Hello, Anne. No, not today. I just dropped by."

At that moment, Libby Fletcher, carrying a large cloth bag, emerged from the back of the shop. "I'm ready," she said to Richard.

Then, seeing me, she broke into a radiant smile, "Oh, how nice to see you, Mistress Shakespeare. Mr. Quiney is walking with me to the market. I promised to bring things home to mother, and he has offered to carry them for me."

I looked at Richard with a raised eyebrow, and he simply grinned at me, with an impudent expression that said, "I may have had no luck with you, Anne, but no harm in trying."

I decided to keep an eye on the situation if I could, and alerted George Camden to do the same. "Libby is a lovely girl, but naive and inexperienced," I told him, "and she won't know how to cope with Richard. Now that she is in our shop, I feel I should look after her."

When I saw the two of them together another day in the high street, Libby looking up at Richard in glowing admiration, I decided to call on Rebecca.

I learned that Richard often visited Libby.

"Now, Rebecca," I said firmly, "I want you to be aware that Richard Quiney is not a proper person to be going about with your granddaughter. He is not a trustworthy man."

She looked at me with astonishment. "But he is such a fine gentleman. He is ever so kind to me, and to Libby too."

"He is much too old to be courting her."

"Oh, but it's not like that at all, I'm sure. I know he is some thirty years of age. He told us that. And he has said nothing to Libby about—that is—"

"Yes, I'm sure he has not. I merely want you to be on your guard, Rebecca. Perhaps you will mention this to Libby, too?"

"Oh, yes, to be sure I will do that." But she looked to me more puzzled than concerned, as I bid her goodbye.

At last, I confronted Richard himself. He gave me a look of astonished innocence. "I don't know what you mean, Anne. Libby is a very pretty girl, but I have no designs upon her, I assure you."

Then George decided it was time to alert Nate Fletcher. "It was like lighting a fire to a cannon," he laughed, reporting to me. Nate shook his fist, raved, and swore he would kill Richard if he so much as touched a hair of Libby's head. Evidently he told Richard the same thing, and that did the trick. Richard went off to London with Edward Bushell, and some time later, we were pleased to hear that Libby was engaged to a handsome young merchant in the town and had left the glover's shop to prepare for her marriage.

V

Meanwhile, Will had finished his new play. It was called *Love's Labours Lost*, and if I had wanted a picture of the life Will had enjoyed in the society of the Earl and his courtiers, here it was in the play, with its charming and superficial characters, clever and idle.

Will gave me the pages to read as he went along. I was

surprised at how rapidly he wrote, with remarkably few corrections or revisions. "It's all there in my head," he explained. "While I'm out walking, I plan out exactly what I want to say. Then it's just a matter of putting it down."

If I had ever doubted Will's genius, that off-hand remark convinced me, as nothing had ever done before, that he was no ordinary mortal when it came to writing.

I couldn't help being amused by the play. The young King of Navarre asks three of his courtiers to join him in a vow to spend three years devoted to serious study, during which time they would see no women, eat sparingly, and shorten their sleep. The others agree, but one of the courtiers protests that while he subscribes to three years' study, he isn't so sure about not seeing any women for that length of time. However, he agrees to join the others and signs the decree, but then reminds the King that the first article, rejecting women, must be broken by the King himself. Has he forgotten that the daughter of the King of France is on her way to Navarre on a diplomatic mission from her ailing father? Oh, dear, the King has indeed forgotten, and of course the Princess cannot be turned away.

And so the beautiful Princess arrives with her three lovely ladies-in-waiting, and in no time at all, the King and his courtiers have abandoned their vows and are all quite madly in love. The ladies are equally smitten, and as I read these passages, filled with the banter that flies among them, I saw clearly the atmosphere that Will loved so much in the group surrounding the young Earl. It was all witty and amusing, and I had to admit that if I had been there and found myself lionized by this elegant company, I would certainly have been flattered, as Will was.

However, as the play went on, I found that after a time the triviality could get pretty tiresome. In the end, when some rustic characters attempt to put on a play to entertain the aristocrats, the lords and ladies amuse themselves at the expense of the bumpkins with such arrogance and cruelty that I felt disgusted.

I said something of this to Will, when we were sitting in our favorite corner of the garden, adding that nevertheless I was impressed that he had been accepted in that very exalted society.

He gave a snort, and surprised me by the bitterness in his voice. "Don't think for a moment, Anne, that I am treated as a *social* equal by these people. They take up with anyone who can amuse them—poets, artists, sometimes servants, who become favorites until their novelty wears away. We have the illusion of being on intimate terms with them, sometimes are literally so. But that's as far as it goes."

He stood up and paced back and forth, scowling. "I'm going down to the river." But as he left for his walk, he tossed over his shoulder a remark that astonished me. "You're worth the lot of them, Anne."

That was Will, all right. Just as I began to wonder about him, he said something that made me feel he had read my mind. And maybe he had.

While he was writing his play, Will had been cheerful, but once it was finished, it was the old story again. He took to staring into space, snapping at everyone, and being generally irritable, and when he had gone, we all breathed in relief.

vi

It must have been a week or so after Will had gone that I made a startling discovery. In tidying up the stacks of books and papers he had left, I found a packet filled with poems. It was stuffed under some discarded pages and looked as if Will must have forgotten it. As I began to look over the pages, I saw that each one contained a poem of fourteen lines in the popular sonnet form. Will had often joked that all lovers were prone to writing sonnets. Now it appeared that during the past year Will had written not a few but dozens of them and had said not a word about it.

I saw that these must have been working copies. Sometimes words or whole lines were blotted out and changed. They were certainly not written at a sitting, because the inks varied frequently.

As I read, I was first struck by the dazzling quality of the verse. I wondered why all the secrecy. but it wasn't long until I saw what the problem was. When I got beyond the first group, I came across some revelations that were pretty startling, to say the least.

The sonnets were not numbered but at times they fell into a pattern that suggested a sequence. The poems began innocently enough. Many were addressed to a young man whom the poet is urging to marry and to produce a son, so that his death will not be the end of his beauty. "Die single, and thy image dies with thee." Then the poet promises immortality through the verse he writes:

But thy eternal summer shall not fade,
So long as man can breathe, or eyes can see,
So long lives this, and this gives life to thee.

But soon there was a change. The poet loves the young man and glows with pleasure that his love is returned:

When, in disgrace with fortune and men's eyes,
I all alone beweep my outcast state . . .
Yet in these thoughts myself almost despising,
Haply I think on thee—and then my state,
Like to the lark at break of day arising
From sullen earth, sings hymns at heaven's gate. . . .

Presently there is a hint that a lady is pursuing the young man. Then comes the revelation that the poet is in love with her too! Oddly enough, nothing more is heard about a lady until the last few pages in the packet.

Meanwhile, dozens of poems follow, ringing the changes on aspects of the poet's love for the young man. Sometimes he refers to his own advancing age:

That time of year thou mayst in me behold
When yellow leaves, or none, or few do hang
Upon those boughs which shake against the cold,
Bare ruined choirs where late the sweet birds sang. . . .

But if he dies, he urges the loved one to grieve only briefly:

No longer mourn for me when I am dead
Than you shall hear the surly sullen bell
Give warning to the world that I am fled. . . .

Now, out of the blue, the woman appears again. She doesn't have the fair complexion which convention requires of ladies. Instead, her hair and her eyes are black. The poet amusingly names some of the traditional attributes of feminine beauty, then turns the tables:

My mistress' eyes are nothing like the sun;

Coral is far more red than her lips' red. . . .
And yet, by heaven, I think my love as rare
As any she belied with false compare.

He loves her desperately. She is to his "dear doting heart" the "fairest and most precious jewel," but she brings him no joy. In truth she is "tyrannous and black" in her deeds. He loathes himself for his weakness, because he cannot resist her charms. The pages came to an end with no solution to the poet's dilemma.

At last I laid down the poems and put them back in the packet.

What to make of all this? I was stunned, and for several days I could think of nothing but the revelations in the sonnets. I had certainly wondered if Will had had a casual episode with a woman now and then, but I didn't expect a serious attachment. I could smile to myself at his obvious infatuation with the young Earl of Southampton. If he wanted to play at being "in love" with the Earl, I could accept that as a poetic convention. It was common enough among the poets of the day for men to express love for one another.

But I was not amused about the "brunette" lady. This was no flirtation. Every word spoke of a passionate sexual relationship. I felt myself burning with anger at the thought of him in bed with this woman, longing for her, hating himself because he couldn't resist her.

I decided to go straight to London and confront him. I would simply turn up at his lodgings. I spent days rehearsing what I would say. I may not be a playwright, but I found I could invent plenty of dialogue to fit that situation. The problem was that I really didn't know what Will would say. Was he still embroiled with this woman? The verses might have been written months ago, or only the day before he left London. What if he simply said, "Sorry, Anne, it's all over with us. I'll send you money and visit the children now and then, but my life will be here in London."

I realized that I simply couldn't take that risk. I'd better wait till he came home and confront him then.

vii

Around this time, I noticed the children were more aware of his absence than ever before. The twins fretted that their friends' fathers stayed at home in Stratford, and why didn't their papa do the same? I reminded them that their papa was a famous actor on the stage, and that was why he must be in London where the theaters were. Susanna, in big-sister fashion, told the twins they should be glad their father had not died, like poor Captain Wilson.

Hamnet nodded his head solemnly. "That's right. David and Agnes don't have a father. At least, Papa comes home when he can."

Well, I thought, not always, but never mind.

Hamnet was growing more like his father every year, with eyes that observed everything, and with a sense of humor that sometimes meant mischief but more often was simply a sense of fun. He was already an outstanding pupil at his school, where learning came easily to him, and he loved nothing more than lying under a tree with a book. Will often took Hamnet on his walks along the river or among the trees in the nearby forest, talking with him about his future, answering his questions about all sorts of things. He delighted in the little girls as well. I watched him with the children and thought again what a fine father he was. My own father had taken little notice of my brother and less of me when we were growing up.

I didn't say a word to Will about the sonnets at first. I would wait till the time was right to bring up that hot topic. He was bursting with news of his own. "I've been made a shareholder in the company! It will mean a good deal more money, and it also means I can come home more often than in the past."

I'll believe that when it happens, I thought. But of course I was pleased at his news. Now he was one of the few who had control of the company, and that was important to him.

That night as we lay in bed, I finally told him that I had read his sonnets.

He looked at me in surprise. "My sonnets? Where did you find them?"

"Stuffed in the bottom of your desk."

There was a long pause. "Oh, I see. And what do you think of them?"

At that, I sat straight up and glared at him. "Do you want a critique, then? The verse is splendid."

I saw an amused smile on his face that infuriated me. "Look here, Will, I don't mind your being infatuated with the Earl. But what about that dark-haired lady?"

At that, Will stepped out of bed and walked over to the window. He stood there for what seemed an age to me. Then he came back and stood beside me.

"I'm sorry you saw that, Anne. I didn't mean to leave them lying about."

"I'm sure you didn't."

"I must have overlooked them."

I fought back tears. "Then you do love her, Will?"

"Oh, my God, no! I despise her. And myself more."

"Do you still see her?"

"No, never. That was all many months ago. She was only a visitor. Everyone around the Earl plays these games. They are not regarded as serious."

"But it was serious to you?"

Now his temper flared. "No, not in the way you mean. These things happen, that's all."

Of course our conversation ended in love-making and that consoled me for the time, but in the days that followed, I understood for the first time how Will had felt all those years ago when he wanted to know about my time with Stephen Brent. Whenever we were alone, I would ask him questions about the dark lady. "Is she beautiful?"

"Yes, many think so."

"Did the Earl care for her?"

"All right, Anne, that's enough."

Still I would ask. "Was she more exciting in bed than I am?"

And so on, until Will finally did as I had done before and refused to answer.

Long afterward I heard someone refer to a friend "sowing his wild oats," and that common phrase brought to my mind that Will was so young when we were married that he'd never had a chance at those oats. Wasn't it inevitable that a man of Will's passionate nature would sow them sooner or later?

Gradually things went back to normal, and soon we all became absorbed in his new play, called *A Midsummer Night's Dream*, full of fun and entrancing poetry. The whole family loved it, and it was at this time that we began what was to become a family tradition. Our children and Rosanna's would copy out lines from Will's plays and perform them as skits. Now Hamnet took the role of Oberon, who tells little David, as Puck, to put the magic juice on Titania's eyes:

I know a bank where the wild thyme blows,
Where oxlips and the nodding violet grows,
Quite overcanopi'd with luscious Woodbine,
With sweet musk-roses and with eglantine.
There sleeps Titania sometime of the night. . . .

And we all applauded when little David played the part of the rustic Bottom wearing an ass's head, while Judith read the lines:

Come, sit thee down upon this flow'ry bed
While I thy amiable cheeks do coy,
And stick musk-roses in thy sleek, smooth head,
And kiss thy fair large ears, my gentle Joy.

Everyone quoted favorite lines, and I felt more and more impressed with Will's genius.

The next year brought an event that the whole family never forgot. For the first time in the eight years since Will had gone to join the acting company, they were coming again to perform in Stratford. Now, to add to the excitement, they were performing Will's new play, called *Romeo and Juliet*, which had opened to great acclaim in London.

It was in the month of July when the company came into town. The players were lodged at the Swan, the finest inn in the town, while Will stayed with us. The play was performed the next afternoon at the Guild Hall, and by three o'clock everybody in town was there, as well as people from all around the area. Rosanna and I sat with our children.

Will's parents were thrilled. Mary sat, gently smiling, while John beamed and chatted with all his old friends. The Quineys were there, old Adrian looking patriarchal, while Richard strolled about, flaunting his good looks. Edward Bushell turned up, dressed in the height of fashion, and George Camden came to sit with us, eager to hear another of Will's plays.

At last the trumpets sounded, and the drums rolled, and the actor came out to speak the Prologue, announcing the story of two households in "fair Verona" who carry on an ancient grudge.

The little boys loved the sword fights, and the little girls were entranced with the young lovers. Presently there was a stir from the audience as people began to recognize Will playing the role of Capulet, Juliet's father. Shouts of "Ho, Will!" were shushed by spectators, and the children were ecstatic.

Everyone sighed when Romeo saw Juliet for the first time:

O she doth teach the torches to burn bright.
It seems she hangs upon the cheek of night
As a rich Jewel in an Ethiop's ear;
Beauty too rich for use, for earth too dear. . . .

And there were more sighs when Juliet stepped out onto her balcony, saying:

Come, gentle night, come loving, black-brow'd night,
Give me my Romeo, and when he shall die,
Take him and cut him out in little stars,
And he will make the face of Heaven so fine
That all the world will be in love with night
And pay no worship to the garish sun. . . .

The audience was riveted with suspense as the story unfolded and moved with breathtaking speed toward the tragic end, with the deaths of the young lovers in the tomb of the Capulets.

In the evening, a reception was held at the inn, where we met and chatted with the players. Richard Burbage told me how valuable Will was to the company, both as actor and as the writer of "those excellent plays." Many others expressed their admiration, and I came away feeling the glow of Will's celebrity.

Later, Will said to me, "You made a great hit with the men, Anne. You're still a handsome woman, you know."

I had been lucky enough to keep my youthful figure, and it pleased Will that people seemed unaware of any difference in age between us.

During the play, I had seen in Romeo the image of the eighteen-year-old Will who had courted me, all those years ago, with such joy at being in love. If I wondered sometimes if he regretted his youthful passion, I believed now that aside from a few dark ladies here and there, I was still the anchor of his life, and that was enough for me.

Watching the play, I had also recalled Will's infatuation with the young Earl of Southampton. Two years had passed since that time, and I had seen that affection change into a genuinely paternal devotion. Will was only ten years older than the Earl, but he had always thought of himself as very much the senior. The Earl seemed to feel the same and regarded Will as a trusted friend, a surrogate father who would always give him wise advice and support.

Now Will told me that the young Earl was in serious trouble with the Queen. At the very time when Will was writing *Romeo and Juliet*, the Earl had met Elizabeth Vernon, an extremely pretty young Lady in Waiting to the

Queen, and had fallen madly in love with her and she with him. This was really playing with fire, for the Queen would allow no courtship of her attendants. It also enraged his guardian, Lord Burghley, who had never forgiven the Earl for rejecting his granddaughter, even though that young woman was now married.

Will knew when he wrote those passages of intoxicating love in *Romeo and Juliet* that they would be most pleasing to the Earl. I laughed and said I had noticed the theme of the young couple marrying for love, defying the wishes of their elders.

Will grinned. "When the Earl saw the performance, he thanked me for that. I believe the Earl and Mistress Vernon do truly love each other, and he will never give her up, whatever the consequences."

Those were prophetic words indeed. There *were* dire consequences in the future, although we didn't know then what they would be.

viii

A few months later, Will managed another visit home. Ten-year-old Hamnet, with his quick wit, his love of fun, and his passion for reading, had become a congenial companion for his father. Will talked with the boy about his school and his plans for the future. He would follow the pattern of the Earl and go to St. John's College at Cambridge and then to the law school in Grays Inn. Of course, they agreed, Hamnet would become a celebrated attorney in London.

Before he left, Will told me about a project he was pursuing. It seems that some years ago, his father had begun to investigate obtaining a coat of arms, a step that would enable him to use the title "Master Shakespeare," the official mark of the status of "gentleman." John had enjoyed that title while Bailiff of Stratford, but had lost it when he was ousted from office. John's early effort to regain the title had been abandoned. Will told me frankly that it was an expensive process and John, having lost much of his holdings, could not afford to go on with it. Of course, the cost was unofficial, but everyone knew that the officers of the College of Arms had to be reimbursed with large sums if the application was to succeed, and now Will planned to make a new application on behalf of his father.

"Why for your father?" I asked.

"It will restore what he lost before. If this succeeds, it confers the status not only on my father but on his sons and all male issue thereafter."

"I see. So you . . . and Hamnet . . . ?"

"Exactly."

"And the money?"

"It's not a problem now." And that was certainly true. Will was earning a substantial income by this time.

The following summer, the plague was so widespread that when the London theaters closed, the company did not go on tour, as the plague was turning up all over the countryside as well. So Will came home for an extended stay. He was working, as always, on a new play, this one titled *The Merchant of Venice*, and as usual he read passages aloud to the assembled family in the evenings. He was nearing the end, coming to the thrilling scene where Portia, disguising herself as a young lawyer, defends Antonio from Shylock's demand for his pound of flesh.

Hamnet, eyes glowing, said, "That's what I shall do,

isn't it, Papa? When I am a lawyer in London, I shall stand in court and defend people."

Will smiled. "Not always, Hamnet. Sometimes you may be the prosecutor."

Susanna frowned. "But only if the cause is right, surely?"

"Let us hope so," said Will wryly.

Now Judith spoke up loyally. "It *will* be a good cause if Hamnet does it!"

Everyone laughed, and I passed round the bowl of toffee candies for our bedtime treat. That tragedy was about to strike seemed utterly remote from our tranquil lives.

The next day, Hamnet slept late and woke up coughing. By the afternoon, the telltale swellings appeared in the groin and under the arms. His whole little body burned with fever, and as the swellings burst, the horrible odor of the plague filled the room. He moaned with pain, and during the night, as Will and I sat with him, he threw himself about, suffering the nightmares of delirium. The doctor came and shook his head. We wrapped him in wet sheets, poured cool water on his burning face, and tried to give him sips of water which he could scarcely swallow. For three days, we watched our child suffering, and by the morning of the fourth day, he was quiet, all consciousness gone. All day, he lay in that somnolent state, and an hour after midnight, our child was dead.

None of that terrible time is clear in my mind. I remember poor Mary on her knees, praying to her saints and weeping for her priest, who could have given absolution to the dying child. I remember the children sobbing, and Will, silent and stricken.

On the 11th day of August in the year 1596 our son, at eleven years of age, was buried in the graveyard of the Holy Trinity Church. I remember trying to comfort the children, especially Judith, who had lost her twin. For a long time, I remember finding my bodice soaking wet, unaware of having wept.

Will was dazed, unable to function. Then one day as I sat in the garden, he threw himself on the grass at my feet, weeping with dry sobs that at last brought him relief.

No one ever knew why the plague would strike as it did. No one else in the family was affected. There were scattered cases in Warwickshire that year. Why our precious son? There were no answers.

For a long time after Will had gone back to London, Susanna and Judith slept with me in our big bed. Then slowly, bit by bit, life takes hold and moves the universe along, and things fall back into place. There is no forgetting. There is only the pain, and ultimately the force of survival.

clear, and on the first day the weather held. Greenaway led the way, followed by two of his packhorses laden with goods. I was next, and the three men brought up the rear.

At Oxford, there was a main road wide enough for carriages to go all the way to London, and I was able to get a place in one of these, for a price that astonished me and reminded me of the novelty of having generous amounts of money to spend. We parted from Greenaway here, since he had to leave the main road and make many stops in towns and villages along the way.

We spent our first night at a comfortable inn, with excellent food and a clean bed, and I thought how pleasant it all was until we woke up the next morning to snow falling and an icy wind blowing. When we came to steep hills, the passengers had to walk, while the horses slipped and struggled. Going downhill was worse, when after a few hours, the snow melted and the road became a river of mud.

That night the driver announced that we could not reach the planned destination before darkness fell, and we must stop at the nearest available inn. The place was dirty, the food dry and half-burnt, and I was forced to share a bed with a young girl who had joined us earlier that day. The bed we were given had obviously been slept in by many travelers before us, and the girl wept and complained that her mother ought never to have sent her on this trip alone. It seemed she was returning a string of valuable pearls to an aunt in London who had demanded their return. I told her not to talk about them to anyone, but the next day, she chattered away about them to the men in the carriage.

The next day it rained heavily, slowing our progress even more. Two gentlemen on fine-looking horses had elected to ride along with us, as there had been rumors that robbers were in the area. Both men were armed with pistols, and we were glad to know they were there. However, in the afternoon, as dusk was falling, the carriage came to a sudden stop and the driver told us to fasten the doors and remain silent. Of course, the girl shrieked in terror, babbling about her pearls until I told her to stop.

Presently, we heard the pounding of hoofs, the doors of the carriage were rattled, and voices shouted "Open up!"

The girl screamed and threw herself at me, sobbing in terror. I knew how she felt. My heart was beating hard in my chest, and it hurt to breathe.

We could hear loud voices, the sound of horses neighing and rearing, and suddenly the crack of pistol shots. We sat in frozen silence. Did the shots come from the robbers or were the shots fired by the men riding along with us?

At last we heard the sound of galloping horses, growing fainter in the distance. Whoops of joy went up in the carriage. The doors were opened, and the driver assured us that the robbers were frightened off by shots of our companions on horseback. We made up a generous purse for our rescuers, the two men modestly disclaiming any heroism, and we jogged on without further excitement.

One of the men in the carriage made the cynical remark that the whole thing might have been a ploy. He had heard of cases where a scene like this was set up in league with others posing as robbers, knowing that the wealthy passengers would reward their rescuers. But the next day we learned that a band of robbers had been captured along the same stretch of the road, so we never knew whether we had been duped or not.

On the third night, our accommodations were comfortable again, and as we neared London the next day, I thought about the times when Will first came home to Stratford from London. With little money, he had often walked for long stretches of the way, sometimes hiring the cheapest horses he could find. Now and then he had slept in a barn, or in the fields, and sometimes he had stopped in flea-infested inns, sleeping on filthy pallets. He had casually mentioned all this but without much complaint, and I realized how much he must have wanted to come home to have endured those miserable journeys. No wonder he didn't run back and forth from London to Stratford as often as I would have liked.

When we came into London the next morning, I was amazed at the masses of people thronging the streets. Horses with well-dressed riders scattered the pedestrians, splashing mud as they came through. Carts carrying all sorts of goods jostled for space in the crowded lanes, and the noise was constant. Hawkers cried out their wares, people shouted, dogs barked. Stratford, even on market day, was never anything like this, I thought. And it went on, street after street, as if it would never end.

At last, after making several stops, the carriage brought me to a spot near St. Paul's Cathedral, the area where Will now had comfortable lodgings. I found a porter to carry my portmanteau, and I followed him to the address I knew so well from sending my letters there for the past year or so.

When we finally reached the house, a dark-haired young woman, wearing a black dress and a red kerchief, opened the door. "Mistress Shakespeare?" she asked.

"Yes. Is my husband at home?"

"Not just now, ma'am," she said.

I wasn't surprised that Will was not there, as he would have had no way of knowing what time I might arrive. It was early afternoon by now. He would be at the theater, probably in rehearsal, as I knew there was no performance that day.

I heard the woman say, "This way, please."

We went up two flights of stairs, the porter following. The woman took out a key, unlocked a door, and walked in ahead of me, to my surprise. Good servants always came in after, not before.

When the porter had put down my things and I had given him the sum he asked for and a bit extra, he thanked me and clattered down the stairs. I turned to see the woman staring at me boldly.

"He'll be back about dusk, most like," she said, her eyes surveying me from head to toe. "Will you be wanting summat to eat?"

No "madam" followed the question, and I gave her a cool stare back.

"Yes, please."

She left, with no curtsey. Well, I thought, if that's city manners, I'm not impressed.

I soon forgot such trivialities, however, when I went to the window and looked out on a scene that dazzled me. So close I felt I could almost touch them stood the massive stones of the cathedral, and if I leaned far out and looked up, I could see the great dome, gleaming in the winter sun. Then straight ahead, the town lay before me, its great river moving under the bridge lined with shops and dwellings, its endless streets that extended far beyond the river, dotted with church spires, and at the end of the bridge, the Tower where prisoners were taken, sometimes never to return.

Presently, a little maidservant arrived with a welcome tray and a shy smile. I placed it on a table by the window, where I could continue to gaze at the panorama laid out before me.

At last I left the window and looked around the three rooms that Will had described to me. In addition to the room with the view, there was a bedroom and a smaller room with a table and chair for his writing. The furnishings were of good quality, not luxurious but much better, Will had told me, than the cheap sticks that had furnished his earlier dwellings.

Finally, I unpacked my bag and stretched out on the bed, where I fell asleep almost at once, and that is where Will found me when he returned from the theater. He lay down beside me and took me in his arms. Then, with a grin, he said, "Let's go for a walk while it is still light. This can wait."

I agreed, eager to see more of this amazing city. We went first into the great cathedral. I had seen etchings and drawings of it, but the reality, looking up into the height of the dome from inside, was beyond my imagining. We strolled in the courtyard, where stalls were set up to sell a bewildering variety of objects, and afterward we walked onto the bridge and stood under the forbidding stones of the famous Tower.

Back in our lodgings, the little housemaid brought up a delicious meal, and at last we snuggled into our bed.

ii

The next day brought me the long-awaited chance to see Will's company in their own theater. Since ladies couldn't appear alone in public, we had arranged for Rosanna's brother, Edward Bushell, to escort me, as Edward happened to be in London at the time.

First, we would see *King Richard II*, a play that I had had serious doubts about when I read Will's copy a year or so earlier.

"Are you sure you ought to be writing about a King who was deposed?" I had asked him then. But he had airily declared that, after the success of his Henry VI and Richard III, he and his fellow owners were keen to go back in time and cover the reigns of the Kings leading up to Henry V. They were confident their loyalty would not be questioned, even though they knew the Queen was obsessed with the fear that after her death, her enemies would regain control of the country, or that worse yet, they would try to depose her while she was still reigning Queen and put a usurper in her place.

Will had to admit that the aging Queen had plenty of reason for such fears. Recently, a pamphlet had been published by a conference of English Catholics meeting in Antwerp, containing a lengthy discussion of whether King Richard II had been justly deposed and concluding that the act *had been justified.* The devastating shock to the Queen was the dedication on the title page of the pamphlet: to "Robert Devereaux, Earl of Essex," suggesting him as a candidate for leadership in case of insurrection.

The handsome Essex was the Queen's current favorite, eclipsing his predecessor, Sir Walter Raleigh. Of course, Essex had rushed to the Queen and passionately disclaimed any knowledge of the pamphlet, but who knew what she believed? And for that matter, who knew whether Essex himself was really as innocent as he proclaimed?

This incident had special significance for Will, because Essex was the mentor and idol of his precious Earl of Southampton, and Will worried that if any trouble arose, his young Earl would follow without question in the footsteps of the charming Essex.

In the light of all this, Will had made every effort in writing the play to give a balanced view of King Richard and the events of his reign. When I read it, I agreed that it certainly didn't read like a propaganda piece for deposing a monarch, but I still wouldn't have touched the subject with a ten-foot pole. Yet the play had been approved by the Court censor, with the proviso that the scene of the actual deposition be removed. Since that time, it had been performed several times with no problems, and had proved popular with the public, so what did I know?

The performance was to begin at the usual hour of three o'clock. Edward called for me in plenty of time, looking very smart, as usual. I was glad I had invested in several handsome gowns for my London visit, getting the seal of approval from Edward, who prided himself on his knowledge of women's fashions.

When we arrived, the theater had already begun to fill with well-dressed patrons finding their way to the tiers of seats covered by the rooftops, while the common people milled about in the ground area that was open to the sky. The weather was remarkably mild for January, with no rain or snow to keep them away.

As the trumpets sounded to announce the time for the play to begin, a group of elegant men and beautifully dressed ladies appeared in the special room just above the stage on the right, which was reserved for titled and highly honored guests. From where I sat, in the second tier, I could see the young man with long golden curls who I knew at once was Will's beloved Earl, and at his side was the extremely handsome man, some years older than Southampton, who must be the Earl of Essex. No wonder the Queen was enamoured, I thought. Although I couldn't hear their conversation, I could see that our young Earl often joined the others in their little private jokes and murmured remarks, but I also noticed that once the performance began, he often ignored them and watched the players with intense concentration.

When I had first read the play, I had questioned whether Richard was so bad that he should be deposed. Would the skill of the actors make this more convincing?

As the play opens, his opponents express their concern that the King's greed and extravagance will bankrupt the country. This is expressed, on his deathbed, by the venerable John of Gaunt, the character played by Will at this performance. I watched eagerly as the old man is carried in on a pallet and Will's voice conveyed the passionate sorrow of the old man, giving a moving tribute to his beloved country:

This royal throne of kings, this scepter'd isle,
This happy breed of men, this little world.
This precious stone set in the silver sea . . .
This blessed plot, this earth, this realm, this England. . . .

Unfortunately, the King's greed leads him to a fatal act. With Gaunt dead, he seizes all the money and the lands that should have come to Gaunt's son, young Henry Bolingbroke, whom Richard had sent into exile.

Bolingbroke, a handsome and popular figure, rushes back to England. All the forces against Richard now join with him to defeat the King's supporters. As Bolingbroke makes his way toward London, he is hailed by the crowds, shouting "Welcome!"

Whilst he, from the one side to the other turning,
Bareheaded, lower than his proud steed's neck,
Bespake them thus: "I thank you, Countrymen!"
And thus still doing, thus he passed along.

During this speech, I felt a shiver when I saw the little group around the Earl of Essex smile and make little bows toward him. If he sees himself as a young Bolingbroke, I thought, this could be serious trouble. Although the actual scene of deposition was omitted, the King was imprisoned and the play ends with his death. I had to admit that the brilliance of the actors made it all more persuasive, but I still had my doubts.

After the final bows, and the acclamation of the spectators, Edward escorted me onto the stage, where the Earls and their party had come down and were standing about, chatting with the players. Will took my arm at once and presented me to his young Earl, who smiled with incredible sweetness and said that he was delighted to see me, as of course Will had so often spoken of me. As we talked briefly about the play, I was instantly in love with this charming young man. He smiled warmly into my eyes with genuine pleasure, before he moved on with his friends, and I was surprised to note that in spite of his long curls, there was not a trace of girlishness about him.

Edward hung about, attaching himself to one of the Earl's party with whom he was acquainted. It won't be long, I thought, before we hear about his dearest friend, the Earl of Southampton. Oh, well, Edward was all right in his way.

After the theater, Edward invited us to dine with him at the splendid tavern where he stayed during his visits to London. "They do a first-rate meal," he said. And he was right, they did.

During dinner, Edward surprised me with his opinion that the deposition of King Richard was quite justified.

"But Edward," I protested, "surely there have been plenty of sovereigns who were equally bad one way or another. Isn't there a value in stability?"

He gave me his supercilious smile. "That's as may be. Besides, in the end, Bolingbroke expresses his deep regret and sense of guilt over deposing King Richard."

That's all very well, I thought, but if I were our present Queen, I wouldn't take much comfort from knowing that if somebody deprived me of my throne, that person would suffer remorse afterward.

Later that evening, Will teased me about my instant infatuation with his young patron.

"He is utterly charming," I said. "Is it affectation? He made me feel he really liked meeting me."

"No, it's quite genuine."

Later, Will opened his letters and gave a snort. "It's that damned pest, Richard Quiney. He wants to borrow money again. A large amount this time! What on earth for?"

"Has he paid it back before?"

"Yes, but not very promptly. I suspect his father must have paid up for him. Now he says this loan will be secured by Edward Bushell. Odd that Edward said nothing about it this evening."

"Poor Edward. He seems to be the victim of Richard's so-called charm and probably doesn't want to admit that Richard exploits him. Will you lend him anything?"

Will snorted. "Not a chance. He'll have to find another victim."

I couldn't help feeling a delicious sense of triumph that after all those years of Richard Quiney patronizing Will, he was now reduced to asking Will for money.

For the next two days we saw the two parts of *King Henry IV*, continuing the saga. As the play begins, we find that Bolingbroke, now Henry IV, is not a happy man. Rebellions against him are threatened, and he is in despair over his son, young Prince Hal, who takes no responsibility for his future as heir to the throne, but hangs about with a fat and disreputable old Knight named Sir John Falstaff. The scenes with Falstaff were hilarious, and he had become so popular a figure by this time that the spectators roared and applauded each time he came on.

When Falstaff and the disreputable characters around him plan to rob some travelers on the highway, I shivered, remembering all too well my own brush with robbers.

Everyone loved the scene where Falstaff and Prince Hal take it in turn to play the role of the King, admonishing his son for his irresponsible behavior. And at the end of the second play, the audience groaned in despair when the young Prince, having reformed and repudiated his evil ways, sees Falstaff and utters the fatal words, "I know thee not, old man."

Not only were the audiences devastated that they would see no more of Falstaff, the Queen herself, when the plays were performed at the Court, also wanted to see more of Falstaff. She summoned Will to her presence and asked for another play featuring the old reprobate. A "request" from Her Majesty was a command, and Will reluctantly tossed off what he regarded as a bit of nonsense titled *The Merry Wives of Windsor.* Elizabeth was duly grateful, and, as the future proved, it was always a good thing to be in her favor.

I noticed that Will had mixed feelings about the Queen. He was glad that she was a great patron of the theater and usually managed to counteract the Puritan factions when they tried to convince the public that the theater was a corrupter of morals. Moreover, he admired the Queen for her intelligence. "She speaks several languages, you know," he said one day, "and she has a powerful intellect. She holds her own with the rulers of other nations, and that's no mean accomplishment."

"So what are her shortcomings?" I asked.

He frowned. "She can be unpredictable and cruelly unfair at times. She is usually shrewd in her handling of state affairs, but she is vulnerable to handsome men, who of course flatter her, and this can result in bad decisions for the country. Her problem is that she is vain of her appearance, and she cannot face it that she is growing old."

I said no more, but it seemed to me it must be hard for anyone who has such absolute power to keep any kind of balance. That's the problem with all those monarchs, I thought. No one dares to disagree. Everyone fawns on them. How can they ever know who to trust? How do they ever know who is really a friend?

As the days went by, Will was often at the theater, and Edward took me about the town when the weather was decent. One day, when he called for me, the woman in the red kerchief admitted him and watched us, with her bold stare, as we were leaving.

"Who is that woman?" Edward asked. "I don't like her manner."

"Neither do I," I said. "Her husband is the landlord. He seems pleasant enough, but she is very strange."

Then one day, when Will and I were standing in the vestibule, ready to leave, the woman said, "Good morning, sir," in a voice so different from her usual coldness that I was startled. And then she reached up with her hand and brushed off the collar of Will's coat.

He turned and said sharply, "That will do," and led me quickly out the door.

I gave him an inquiring look, and he muttered, "That woman is a damned nuisance."

"Well," I said, "she seems to take a proprietary interest in you."

He turned and glared at me, his voice shaking with anger. "I can't help that, Anne." His manner turned sullen, and he didn't speak again until we reached the theater.

I noticed that I saw very little of the red kerchief after that. The little housemaid did everything that was required for me during my stay.

It was pretty obvious to me that Will must have plenty of women like this one who were available to him if he wanted them. A handsome and famous actor, with a wife far away in the country, was fair game indeed. I saw that in this case, Will didn't seem to care for the approaches of his landlord's wife, but how many others might there be who were more attractive to him?

It was a problem I had faced after the episode of the dark-haired lady of the sonnets, and I had accepted that there might be affairs from time to time. Now I realized that that was all very well in the abstract, but being here in London made it painfully real.

So what could I do about it? Asking Will would be useless. What could he do but deny it? Eyeing every woman we met with a question would accomplish nothing. I had seen his fury at even a hint of suspicion on my part.

In the end, I saw that so long as Will seemed devoted to our life in Stratford, there was no point in creating trouble. I didn't like it, but I accepted it.

During those two weeks, Will spoke of Hamnet's death and acknowledged that his work was a boon for him. It required so much concentration and activity that it filled up the hours. For me, the distractions of the visit had also been a godsend, but the pain was always there.

In the end, I was ready to go back to Stratford. London

was indeed an exciting place, but I noticed that the incessant noise went on through much of the night, and I yearned for a little peace and quiet. Will thrived on the constant activity, but I was geared to a slower pace. In London, he was intensely preoccupied and often irritable. By the time I arrived home, I was beginning to think that the pattern of our lives, with Will coming and going at long intervals, was not so bad after all.

iii

In the month of May, Will came home and dropped a shocking surprise. On the first afternoon, he asked me to take a walk with him, and presently he stopped in front of a splendid house in Chapel Street, still known to the locals as "New Place," although it had been built more than a century earlier.

Will asked casually, "How would you like to live here, Anne?"

"Here? At New Place? Are you joking?"

Now he smiled broadly. "I hope you'll like it, because it's ours!"

"Oh, Will! It's wonderful! But it must have cost a great deal of money?"

"It did. But we can afford it now."

It was a grand house indeed. Constructed of brick and timber, it was over sixty feet across, with five gables. There's a grassy courtyard between the street and the house and an enormous garden across the back. Will stayed for weeks, while he ordered repairs and we selected fine furniture for many parts of the house. Elegant beds—those symbols of wealth—were ordered, the finest for John and Mary, the second-best bed for us, and pretty ones for each of the girls. Will's special obsession was the back garden, where he planted his favorite shrubs and flowers, making paths through the shrubbery and creating little dells with fountains and stone benches. No one could have imagined then that this innocent garden would one day be the scene of a brutal murder.

Finally, Will supervised our move from the house in Henley Street. His coat of arms had been granted in the preceding November, so everything was now done for Master and Mistress Shakespeare, for John and Mary as well as ourselves, and John loved having his title restored.

One day, we were standing with his mother at the front of the house, when Will said, "Well, mother, I believe it's finer than your family home at Wilmcote, is it not?"

Mary glowed with pleasure. "It is indeed!"

On the night before Will went back to London, we walked together to the churchyard. The moon was hidden by clouds, and only a lone star or two glimmered from the dark sky. We stood silently before Hamnet's little grave.

Will said, "It would all have been good for him, would it not? A fine home. *Master* Hamnet Shakespeare. University. Inns of Court."

"Yes," I said. "It would have been good."

He took my hand, and we walked slowly back to Chapel Street. At the front gate, looking up at our grand new home, I said, "It's lovely, Will."

"Yes," he said. "So it is."

When Will had gone, I found myself pondering a question that puzzled me. Why had Will decided to purchase this grand house and invest in all its lavish furnishings? Will had never shown the least sign of social snobbery, nor was he given to boasting about either his accomplishments or his obviously growing wealth. So why all this?

First, I remembered his remark to Mary about her childhood home. Will truly loved his mother, and I believe he wanted to make up to her for those years when John had lost his position in the town, along with his courtesy title of "gentleman." Now, that title was restored, and she was living in a house that matched that of her upbringing.

Then I remembered Will saying that several of his fellow shareholders in the company had fine country houses where they spent much of their time out of London. Was he trying to "keep up" with his peers? Somehow, it didn't seem like Will. I was certain that he would not go back to London and boast about his new property. More likely, he wouldn't mention it to anyone.

So why? I decided in the end that all this was simply what seemed fitting to himself. He believed in his own talent, he believed that he had earned the fame and fortune that had come to him, and when he saw that this fine house was available and he could now afford it, he bought it. Not to boast, not to compete with others, but simply to do what he himself liked. It was a part of that same spirit that had inspired him, at the age of eighteen, to take me for his wife. That's what he wanted, and he saw no reason not to have it.

Once we were settled in, old John cheerfully shifted the Saturday evening gatherings to the new house, where we sat around the fire in the ground floor parlor, with John as the genial host. It was there one evening that Richard made the startling announcement that his son Thomas was coming to live in Stratford!

Nate Fletcher looked bewildered. "Didn't know you had a son, Richard." One or two others expressed the same surprise, and someone asked, "How old is the boy?"

Richard looked at me. "How old would he be now, Anne?"

"Well," I said, in a scathing tone, "Susanna is fifteen, and little Tom was born soon after that, as you may remember, Richard."

Unabashed, Richard nodded. "Yes, to be sure, of course. Fifteen."

He explained that the boy had been living with his maternal grandparents far away in the north. Now, they had both died and Tom was coming here to Stratford.

One of the men said, "Well, Adrian, you'll soon have a grandson with you."

Richard's father ran a hand through his white locks and grinned. "So it seems."

It was pretty obvious that Richard was not overjoyed at the prospect of having this boy turn up out of the blue. From the day Richard was born, Adrian had doted on him, giving him anything he wanted, bailing him out of debt, forgiving his peccadilloes, and always beaming with pride at his handsome and charming son. Was Richard afraid that his father might transfer some of that worship to his grandson? Richard still lived at home with his father, and the boy would naturally live in their household. Would his presence also inhibit Richard's freedom?

Later that evening, Richard said to me, "I'm counting on you to look after young Tom when he comes. You are so good with children, Anne."

"Never mind the flattery, Richard," I said. "Of course I'll be kind to the boy, but he is *your* responsibility, and don't you forget it!"

When I wrote the news to Will, I said I wondered if Tom would be a chip off the paternal block. "All we need is another Richard."

But when the boy came, that was not the problem. He

was as different from his father as I could have wished.

Richard brought him to my door, saying, "Here's Tom, Anne." And to his son, "This is Missus Shakespeare. I must be off. Be a good boy!"

I saw a slender boy with dark eyes that were a sad reminder of his pretty mother. "Papa thinks I am a child," he said with a shy smile.

I smiled back and took him into the small parlor, where Susanna and Judith did their best to make him feel welcome. He did not talk readily, but after a time, their friendliness helped him to feel more at ease. He told us about his grandparents, who had been good to him. The grandfather had died several months ago from a bad heart, and then his grandmother caught a chill and was quite suddenly gone. He struggled to hold back his tears, and the girls chattered to each other for a bit, giving him time to recover.

I asked about the countryside where he lived. "We were on the edge of a great lake called Windermere, and there are hills and trees everywhere."

Judith asked, "Did you swim in the lake?"

"Oh, yes, in the summer. And we had a boat."

Susanna asked if he went to school there, and he said, "Yes, but I left before the end. The ones who were the good scholars could finish the course and go on to university, but I didn't care for that."

That put a brief pause in the discussion, as both girls were keen on reading and loved their lessons. I quickly filled the gap by asking if he was pleased to meet his father for the first time?

His dark eyes glowed. "It is what I have longed for all my life. He is so handsome, and such a wonderful person, is he not?"

Tom was sitting next to me, with his hand on the arm of

the chair. To avoid a direct answer, I put my hand over his and gave him a warm smile. "I hope you will be very happy here, Tom."

"Thank you. I'm sure I will."

The girls took him for a walk in the garden, pointing out the paths and dells that we were just becoming familiar with ourselves. We invited him to join us at dinner and were surprised to hear his eager questions about our local parish church. What were the penalties for persons who did not attend? Was the incumbent a rector or a vicar? What punishments were inflicted for those who committed offenses?

I was aware that my answers to these questions were a bit vague, and I said, "I am surprised at your asking about these matters, Tom. Most young gentlemen don't seem to take much interest in the church."

Now he looked shocked. "Is that true? It is very different at my home. My grandfather was a deacon, and it was important to everyone in our community that the moral standards of the church be upheld."

Susanna choked into her napkin and Judith bent to the floor to pick up an imaginary object. The girls were well aware of the rumors of Richard's behavior, in general if not in detail. I gave them each a reproving glance. Then I looked at Tom and felt a pang. He had noticed nothing, and his sensitive face, with the serious expression in his dark eyes, made it clear that any view of the world other than the one he held was inconceivable to him. I could see nothing but trouble and heartache in the future if Richard didn't change his ways.

After dinner, the boy left, with many thanks, and the girls walked the short distance with him to his new home, where he told them how eager he was to become acquainted with his father.

Judith expressed her concern. "Poor Tom. He seems young for his age, doesn't he?" Even at thirteen, Judith felt herself to be more mature than Tom's fifteen. "But he is a dear boy. I hope Richard will be kind to him."

Susanna frowned. "What will happen when he learns more about his father?" I wondered the same, and the first episode wasn't long in coming.

On the first Sunday after Tom's arrival, Richard and Adrian came to church with Tom, introducing him to the Rector and having him registered by the parish clerk as a new communicant. Tom was impressed with the size and what seemed to him the grandeur of our local Holy Trinity Church. Although its original paintings on walls and ceiling had been whitewashed after the Reformation, as they now called the changeover to Protestant rule, the church was still a fine structure, far grander than the one where Tom grew up. Of course, everyone in Stratford was there, as church attendance was mandatory, and fines were levied on those who missed for one reason or another. People like Richard had always cheerfully paid his fines whenever he didn't bother to attend. After all, as he said, the fines constituted good income for the church.

So the first Sunday went well for Tom. The following week, Richard airily announced that he had business out of town and would not attend, and poor Tom was shocked. "But he cannot do business on the Sabbath," Tom had protested to his grandfather, and Adrian had evidently shrugged and told him to take no notice.

We heard this from Tom after the service, when he came along with us to our dinner. "Does my father do this often?" he asked me. And I saw no point in not telling him the truth, as he would learn it soon enough. "I'm afraid he does, Tom."

Bewildered, he asked, "But isn't he punished?"

"I believe the fine is increased if it happens too often."

When Richard came along in the evening, Tom asked him at once about the matter, and was told not to worry, the fines were not too steep.

"But, Papa, it is not a matter of money, but of the state of your soul!"

Richard stared at the boy, then burst out laughing. "Well, well, we have a young Puritan among us!" and when it was time for them to go, he put his arm around Tom's shoulder and walked home with him.

Surprisingly, Richard did attend church more often for quite some time after that, and I had a faint hope that things might change.

iv

At about this time, Will wrote the good news that the Earl of Southampton seemed to have gained favor with the Queen. Now a young man of twenty-four, he had been anxious for some time to go abroad in the Queen's service, but had been refused because of his family's obvious Catholic connections. Now the Earl of Essex had been restored to the Queen's favor, and was being sent on an expedition to the Azores against Spain, and his protégé, the Earl of Southampton, had at last been given a chance for service. On this first outing, Southampton returned a hero. His vessel had fought and successfully sunk a Spanish man-of-war, while Essex had failed miserably, allowing the main part of the Spanish fleet to escape without a fight.

Will was delighted. Now the Earl had been rewarded with a new assignment. He was named to accompany Lord

Cecil to France, a gratifying mark of trust. The aging Queen adored Southampton, probably seeing in him the charming son she had never had. The mission was to persuade the King of France not to make peace with Spain, and the English delegation remained at the French court for many months in a vain effort to succeed.

Unhappily for Southampton, he learned a few months later that as a result of their passionate farewell on the eve of his departure, his beloved mistress, Lady Elizabeth Vernon, was expecting his child.

I was in London again when this news reached Will in the form of a letter from the Earl asking Will for a very great favor. Would Will be kind enough to take a secret message to his Lady? If he, the Earl, wrote to her directly, the letter might be intercepted. The message named a date a week later when his beloved must go to a certain small church in a rural area not far from London. She would understand. And of course, so did we.

Will said that as he himself might be recognized if he called upon the lady, perhaps I would be willing to visit her to deliver this message? Of course I would!

On the pretext of a message from Will concerning a play, I presented myself at the home of Lady Rich, the sister of the Earl of Essex, where Elizabeth Vernon was staying, and was admitted without question. In no time, an enchantingly pretty young lady appeared. "You come from our friend Master Shakespeare?"

I told her who I was and, making sure we were not overheard, I gave her my message.

Glowing with joy, she led me to a sofa and sat beside me, taking my hands in hers and looking into my eyes. "You know about—?"

"Yes, my dear. How many months—?"

A faint flush touched her cheeks "I am in the sixth month. I've concealed it till now, as you see." She indicated the full skirts and jacket she wore. "But soon Her Majesty will know—and I am so frightened, not for myself but for Henry."

Henry? I thought, then remembered the dedication to Will's *Venus and Adonis*: "To Henry Wriothesley, Earl of Southampton," etc.

"Why is the Queen so opposed to your marriage? Surely she must see that a lovely young lady like you will inevitably wish to marry?"

"Yes, but you see, it is a very great honor to be selected as a Lady in Waiting, and we are all required to vow not to marry until she chooses to release us. We have many duties to perform and it takes much time for us to learn how to do these properly. She does not like to lose one of her Ladies too soon."

"I see. And how long have you been in her service?"

"Just two years."

I smiled. "I have a daughter only a few years younger than you, my dear, and I should not like to see her so restricted."

Her eyes filled with tears. "My mother would have felt the same, I know, but she died when I was twelve. You are so kind, Mistress Shakespeare."

"My name is Anne," I told her, and in that moment, I became her surrogate mother. She poured out to me how much she loved her Henry, how happy she was to be having his child, in spite of the problems it brought, and how excited she was that within the week, they would be man and wife. When I rose to go, she threw her arms around me. "Thank you, Mistress Anne! Thank you for coming!"

I walked slowly back toward Will's lodging, content with my errand, when suddenly I felt my arms seized by two men, one on either side. I called out for help, but they hustled me quickly into a nearby doorway and down a long corridor to a room with a barred window high up the wall.

"What do you want?" I protested. "I have no money."

They pushed me into a chair, and the taller one, a fierce-looking brigand, growled, "We don't want your money. We want to know what message did you take to Essex House? And you may as well tell us if you want to get out of here."

I was terrified, knowing only too well that people who displeased the Queen were often brutally dealt with. Then, it came to me that if I showed my fear, it could only make matters worse. I decided to try another approach. If it didn't work, it couldn't be worse than it was now.

I gulped and hung my head as if embarrassed. "It's about my husband."

"Master Shakespeare, him that writes them plays and acts on the stage?"

I let my head droop. "Yes, that's the one."

"So what did you tell 'em there?"

I squirmed in my chair and finally said, "There's a lady there that's too friendly to my husband when I'm not about. I went to ask her to leave him alone."

The man broke into a loud laugh, and his companion chortled. "Can't the man look after hisself? We'll see what *he* has to say."

Now I clasped my hands and began to sob. "Oh, sir, please. He doesn't know I went to see her. Please don't tell."

They looked at each other and shrugged. "She don't know nothink. Let her go," said the taller one. And they left me to find my way out.

When I told Will I had been followed and questioned, he blamed himself for letting me go alone. But when he heard my story, he had to laugh. "Too bad women can't be actors," he said, "or we'd put you in the company."

Then I told him I thought Elizabeth Vernon was the perfect mate for the Earl. "Do you think the Queen will relent for these two?"

Will shook his head. "She is getting more irascible every year. No one knows what she will do."

Privately, I had to believe that the Virgin Queen, as she was known, whether truly a virgin or not, must feel some envy of young couples in love and was glad enough to enforce the existing rules against them. And so it proved. When the Queen learned that her Lady in Waiting had married without her permission, she was furious and sent her to Fleet Street prison as an example to others not to break the rules.

I was relieved to learn that she was not placed in a cell like common prisoners but was given quarters where she could have her own furnishings and her maidservant.

Now Southampton was recalled in disgrace from France and sent to the same prison, but it was little consolation to either of them, for they were not allowed to meet. He could not even be with her when she gave birth to their daughter, and it was many weeks later before they were both released and could at last take up their lives together.

Well, I thought, so much for the Earl's favor at Court, which had seemed so promising for his future. That didn't last long.

V

Back in Stratford, life went on as usual. Now that we had moved to our elegant house on Chapel Street, Rosanna and I and our children no longer had the convenience of our adjoining gardens. Still, it was only a ten-minute walk between us, and we continued to meet almost daily.

Young Tom Quiney had found an occupation for himself. It began when he offered to help the sexton at the church, who was responsible for keeping the building and grounds in good order, digging graves, and performing other tasks. Tom loved being a part of church life, and he became so valuable to the sexton that he was eventually hired and given a small stipend for his work.

Tom never seemed to give up on his hero worship of his father. One day he came to me, looking troubled. It seemed that a very pretty lady had been staying at their house, and one night Tom saw her in her nightdress going into Richard's bedroom. Surely that was not proper, was it?

I said, "Have you asked your father about this, Tom?"

"Oh, yes, and he laughed and said the lady had thought she heard a prowler and had been frightened and had come to him for help."

"I see. Then, that seems to explain it, doesn't it?"

Tom frowned. "But why wouldn't she call one of the servants first? And besides, she didn't look frightened at all. She was smiling at Papa. I am so afraid that she is a wicked woman who will lead him into temptation, as it says in the Bible. I have been praying for him."

It was not long after that when Tom reported that his father sometimes stayed at a house he owned around the corner on Wood Street. The tenant had left and Richard was presumably having improvements made before letting it again.

Poor Tom, I thought. A few more episodes and even this innocent will begin to understand. But a few months later, events took a startling new turn.

I was sitting on the terrace of our house, looking out into

the garden, when Rosanna arrived and sat down beside me.

"I have something to tell you, Anne."

She was usually so placid that I was surprised to see she was obviously stirred by some keen emotion. "Is something the matter?" I asked.

Now her face flushed, and she gave me a wavering smile. "No. It's just that Richard Quiney has asked me to marry him!"

I've never been given to shrieking when startled, but I can tell you I came close to it that time. Gathering myself together, I said calmly, "And have you given him an answer?"

"No. I wanted to talk to you about it first."

Well, I thought, it was obvious that if she meant to refuse him, she wouldn't need to ask me. She would simply have said no. Which meant that she wanted me to approve. And how could I? Rosanna was a wealthy woman, and Richard was chronically in debt. Rosanna was a serene and gentle person, and I could see nothing but pain and heartache in such a marriage. She had a quiet beauty, with the olive skin and dark eyes of her Italian mother, and a face like a madonna. She also had a voluptuous body, of which she seemed to be quite unaware, but Richard certainly wouldn't have missed it. In fact that brought me to wonder why this hadn't happened before.

"Rosanna, is this the first time Richard has—er, that is—approached you?"

"No. He sort of hinted at something once or twice, but I wasn't ready to think of such a thing then."

"But now you are?"

"I'm not sure, Anne. He seems to care for me very much. He is quite passionate about it." And a painful flush rose again on her cheeks.

So that was it. How could I not understand? Rosanna

had lost her husband after only a few short years of marriage, and during much of that time he had been away at sea. She had been alone for years. Why should she not want the pleasures of love and marriage? If only it wasn't Richard. Too bad I hadn't told her about Richard's overtures to me, but he was her brother's friend and I hadn't wanted to distress her. Too late now. Still, I had better try.

Softly, I said, "Rosanna, you must have heard gossip from time to time about Richard and various women. This might prove to be a problem for you if you married."

Now she gave me a glorious smile. "Oh, Anne, Richard tells me that he has had many lady friends since his wife died so long ago, but he has never truly loved anyone but me."

Oh, dear. She believed him. Desperate, I tried another tack. "What about the children, Rosanna? Will it be difficult for them to accept Richard as a father?"

"They really do not remember their father. They were too young. I should think it might be fine for them to have a father, don't you?"

Not if it's Richard, I thought. But who knows? Maybe Richard would be all right with her children.

"And what about Richard's son?"

Rosanna smiled warmly. "Tom is such a fine boy. Of course I should want him to live with us, if he wishes to."

One more try. "Rosanna, dear, are you aware that Richard is often in debt? I believe George Camden handles your affairs. It might be wise to consult with him about protecting your money."

She was sure this wasn't necessary, and in the end, I gave up. Two weeks later, Rosanna Wilson and Richard Quiney were married, and the children stayed with us while the couple made a brief trip to Siena to visit her cousin Carla and the Count.

Rosanna's children were surprised, but had no reason to dislike their Uncle Edward's friend Richard. Agnes knew vaguely of Richard's reputation, but she and Susanna talked it over and felt sure that once he was married to lovely Rosanna, all that would be resolved. He had always been pleasant to all of them. Agnes did balk at calling him "Papa," but she and David cheerfully agreed to address him as "Uncle Richard."

When the bridal couple returned, all seemed to go well in the household. We had a direct access to information through the children and heard no complaints. Agnes and Susanna, now young ladies of seventeen, never hesitated to comment on the behavior of the adults, while Judith, at fifteen, would hear the news from David. In the three years since Hamnet's death, Judith had made David a substitute for her lost twin, and David, with his mother's gentle nature, had become her loyal friend.

As for Tom Quiney, he announced that he was fond of his grandfather and did not want to leave him alone in the house, and Adrian had seemed pleased.

Meanwhile, Will's company had pulled off a remarkable coup in London. The lease on the land of their present theater, called the Globe, was due for renewal, but the owner was making unreasonable demands. James Burbage, who had managed the company successfully for so many years, had recently died and his son Richard took over the reins. Now they discovered a clause in the original lease that said that if it was not renewed, the theater could be pulled down. Tired of constant attacks from the Puritan factions, the owners leased a plot of land south of the River, where the Puritans had little influence.

Then came the dramatic event that stunned the city. Making sure the owner was safely out of town, Burbage brought a group of sixteen carpenters and building experts to the Globe on a freezing night in December. With the ground covered in a blanket of snow, the men carefully dismantled the building and conveyed the cargo across the river before daylight. Originally built on the timberframe method, in which pieces of lumber were fitted together with special identifying marks, the joiners were thus able to reconstruct the entire theater when it reached its new location.

The members of the company chortled with glee, and the outraged owner was amply repaid for his greed. Some weeks later, the newly rebuilt Globe was ready to open, and of course it was a new play by William Shakespeare that was announced for the big event.

I went to London for the grand opening, and saw what I consider the greatest of all Will's history plays, *King Henry V*. At the end of *King Henry IV*, we had seen the young Prince Hal promise his father to give up his degenerate way of life. Now it appears that he has kept that promise and has become a strong leader of his country. The Dauphin of France has insulted him with a gift of tennis balls instead of the usual gifts of value, and Henry resolves to conquer the French. "Now all the youth of England are on fire," as they prepare for the expedition to France. On the night before the great battle of Agincourt, the King, disguised in a long cloak, walks among his troops, talking with the common soldiers, reflecting on the fearful odds they will face next day. And who could ever forget the stirring speech he makes in the morning, to rally the hearts of his soldiers?

This day is called the feast of Crispian:
He that outlives this day, and comes safe home,
Will stand a tip-toe when this day is named,
And rouse him at the name of Crispian. . . .

The great battle is won, against all odds, and in a charming scene, the King woos the French princess, bringing peace to both countries.

Will didn't often insert lines in his plays to refer to present events, but he did so in this play. In the Prologue to Act V, the Chorus speaks of "How London doth pour out her citizens" to hail the victorious Henry V, and the same might happen "were now the General of our gracious Empress / As in good time he may—from Ireland coming / Bringing rebellions broached on his sword." Everyone knew this referred to the dashing Earl of Essex, who was still in favor with the Queen and had recently been sent to Ireland to quell a serious rebellion there. Essex had made our dear Earl of Southampton his General of the Horse and, to Will's delight, the young Earl had achieved notice for bravery and distinction as a cavalry officer. If Essex should come back with the rebellion "broached on his sword," he would certainly be greeted, like Henry V, with great acclaim, and he would love every minute of it.

This all sounded fine at the time, but it proved to be the first of a series of events that, at the end of the following year, exploded into disaster beyond our wildest imagining.

vi

Months later, back in Stratford, I had my first hint of trouble in Rosanna's marriage. Up to now, everything had appeared to be remarkably serene. In the early months, the girls had giggled over Agnes's report that "they were always kissing," and David had told Judith that Uncle Richard had taken him out shooting for game and was "a decent sort."

Richard went about oozing charm and looking smug. He was often away on "business," sometimes to London or elsewhere, but there were no rumors of other women in his life.

Now, less than a year after the marriage, Rosanna came to me one day, her dark eyes troubled. "I'm afraid I ought to have listened to you, Anne. Richard is becoming very insistent about money. He wants me to sell some of my family's property, and when I object, he becomes very angry."

"Has he spent much of your money already?"

"Yes, I'm afraid so. But now he wants more, to buy some land that he claims will make us a fortune, but the last ones have not done well at all. I must preserve David's inheritance from his father. I went to see George Camden about it, but he tells me that it is too late now. If I had come to him before the marriage, he could have helped, but once we are married, the husband has total control of all his wife's assets. George is very kind, Anne, but it seems he can do nothing."

I felt as helpless as George and could only express my sympathy. I wrote to Will about it, and that was a mistake. As Will told me later, it led to an open quarrel, of all places, on the stage of the theater. Richard had come to the play one day with Edward Bushell. During the conversation afterward on the stage, Will said something to Richard about taking advantage of his wife's money. Richard was furious and snarled at Will, "Look here, Shakespeare, it's none of your affair. If you give me advice, I'll give you some. You're so fond of your pretty boy, the Earl, but what your wife needs is a man who can make her know she's a real woman."

Will may not have been as tall as Richard but, like most actors, he had plenty of physical strength, and he swung a punch at Richard that knocked him down. Richard staggered up and went for him, but men on both sides pulled them apart and Edward took Richard away with him.

When Will told me this, I couldn't help laughing. "Come on, Will," I said, "you can't take Richard seriously," and Will grinned and said, "All the same, I'm not sorry I hit him."

At the end of September in that year, the next step toward tragedy took place. The Earl of Essex returned from Ireland, but not in triumph with "rebellion broached on his sword." He had made a truce with the Irish chief O'Neill, which was probably a sensible step, but the Queen declared openly that his mission was a failure.

Southampton, who passionately supported whatever Essex did, told Will the story of what happened next. Essex made what he later realized was a fatal mistake. Confident that his charm would always prevail with the Queen, he had galloped in his mud-spattered clothes straight to the Palace and burst in upon her in her private quarters, catching her with her hair down, half-dressed. By this time, as Southampton said, she was wrinkled and quite hideous, but still as vain as a girl. Horrified to be seen with her face unpainted and without her wig, and furious at Essex's failure in Ireland, the Queen had him arrested and sentenced him to be held at York House, a mansion on the Thames, in the charge of the Lord Keeper, Sir Thomas Egerton.

Ever faithful, Southampton, with his wife Elizabeth and their child, moved into Essex House for many months and took charge of the affairs of his beloved patron, not endearing himself to the Queen, to say the least.

vii

The next year was 1600, when we went into a new century, and that summer, I took the girls, now seventeen and fifteen, to London for the first time to see Will's new play, *Hamlet, Prince of Denmark.* The play had already been performed several times and was the talk of London. Everyone wanted to see this wonderful play that wasn't about history and wasn't a comedy, but kept you breathless from beginning to end.

And so it did, from the moment when Hamlet sees the ghost of his father, to the end, when he dies, and his friend Horatio says, "Good night, sweet Prince, and flights of angels sing thee to thy rest."

Will and I listened with amusement while the girls talked about it for days. Judith had heard one of the spectators ask why Hamlet hadn't killed King Claudius sooner. "But how did he know the ghost was real?" she asked indignantly, and Susanna added, "Yes. His mother thought he was going mad, because he kept talking to someone who wasn't there."

And Judith said, "I'm sure he really loved Ophelia, but why did he tell her to go to a nunnery?"

Susanna frowned. "I believe he was angry with his mother for marrying his uncle, and that made him say there should be no more marriages. But remember, at the end he said, 'I did truly love Ophelia, and forty thousand brothers could not make up the sum.' "

They chose different parts of the play for their "favorites." Susanna was deeply moved by the lines where Hamlet thinks of taking his own life, but . . .

. . . the dread of something after death,
The undiscovered country from whose bourn
No traveler returns, puzzles the will,
And makes us rather bear those ills we have
Than fly to others that we know not of. . . .

Judith especially liked the part where Hamlet instructed the players to put on a pantomime acting out the way the King had murdered Hamlet's father by pouring poison in his ear.

"And it worked!" she announced gleefully. "The King was terrified, and everyone could see he was guilty!"

I smiled, and quoted the line, "The play's the thing to catch the conscience of the King!" I had no clue then that one day in the future that episode from the play would have a significant role in solving the murder of Richard Quiney.

I told Will I thought *Hamlet* was the finest piece of work he had done and asked him if it seemed that way to him.

"Yes," he said simply. "I believe it is."

We saw other plays during our stay in London, and on one occasion "our" Earl and his wife were there and the girls were enchanted to be presented to them. I noticed that, concerned as he was about poor Essex, it didn't keep the Earl from coming to the theater and enjoying himself.

Late that summer, the Earl of Essex was finally released, but the Queen humiliated him by adamantly refusing to let him come near the Court, and by cutting off his income from a royal grant on importing wine. And that was too much for Essex and his ego. Many of the men who had fought with Essex and Southampton in Ireland formed a loyal band of supporters. Essex knew he was popular with the people, and he was confident he could succeed if he attempted a rebellion, and Southampton remained his loyal aide.

Several months went by, while Essex became more and more obsessed with visions of himself, like Henry Bolingbroke, riding through the streets of London with the sounds of acclaim on all sides.

Will told me later that he was aware of all this but he had

hoped they would never take the final step. Unfortunately, matters heated up rapidly. Supporters of all ranks, from titled aristocrats to wealthy individuals, from both Catholic and Protestant backgrounds—for Essex promised religious tolerance if he gained power—met frequently in a London mansion.

In early February, Will and the other owners of the company were visited by three men. Two were courtiers of Essex, and the third was none other than our friend Edward Bushell, whose generous purse had gained him a welcome among the plotters. What they asked for was so dangerous that I cannot believe to this day that the company consented. They were asked to give a special performance of *King Richard II* in three days' time, and *it was to include the central deposition scene,* the one forbidden by the censor. I said not a word of reproach to Will, then or later, but I knew he had supported the plan. The others were reluctant at first, but the men offered the players a large sum of money, ostensibly because of the "short time to prepare," and it was agreed.

The performance took place on the following Saturday, the 7th day of February, in the year 1601, at the Globe Theater. I had arrived in London the day before and was there when the play began. Essex and Southampton and their friends were conspicuously present, and when Henry Bolingbroke, in the play, made his triumphal return to London, while the people cheered him, many in the audience shouted and looked up at Essex, who modestly bent his head. Certainly, the intent of the performance was to inflame the populace, and everyone knew they were playing with fire. It seemed to me they must have known that Cecil's spies were alert to what was going on. How could they not be? And indeed, as Essex left the theater, he was served with a formal summons to appear at once before the Privy Council.

What happened after that was the final blow to Essex's ambitions. He defied the Council by saying he was too ill to appear, and that night, all his supporters were told to assemble in the courtyard of Essex House. Soon there were several hundred men in the yard, eager to do whatever was needed. Then Sir Thomas Egerton, who had been Essex's jailer, came in with some high officials from the Court, and Essex made his final mistake. He gave the order to seize the group and hold them under armed guard. And now there was no turning back. In the morning, the party set forth to go to St. Paul's Churchyard, where the plan was for Essex to address the citizens and enlist their support, but they soon discovered that the Queen's forces had been tipped off about their plans and had blocked off the streets. Now they were trapped. Then the government soldiers brought up artillery, and in the end, Essex and Southampton and the others surrendered and were sent to prison in the Tower of London.

Will was devastated. He ranted on about how bitter he was toward the Queen for having treated Essex so badly that he was forced into rebellion and how he wished that Southampton had not been involved. "It is certain death for them both, you know," he said.

I had my own opinion about Essex and his ego. No one is "forced" into a rebellion, but I said nothing about that, only expressing my grief over our young Earl.

Now that the coup had failed, Will and the members of the company were quaking in their boots that they could be involved in the treason. In fact, the next day after I arrived, the owners were served with a demand for a representative to appear before the Queen's inquisitors to answer charges related to their special performance of *King Richard II*. After a heated meeting, in which Will admitted that they were sharply divided on who was to blame for this catastrophe, they had decided to send the actor, Alexander Pope, whose calm demeanor and air of reliability would, they hoped, make a favorable impression.

And fortunately it did. Pope argued that the play had been written and produced four years earlier and had no political intention, and that it was only the large sum of money offered that had induced the company to comply with the request. A substantial fine was levied, which they paid gladly, knowing they had had a lucky escape.

The trial for treason took place the following day in Westminster Hall, the very place where Richard II's deposition had taken place. The evidence against the conspirators could not be disputed, and the inevitable guilty verdicts were recorded for many, including Essex and Southampton. Will and I were among the spectators when their sentence was read aloud:

"You both shall be led from hence to the place from whence you came, and there remain during Her Majesty's pleasure; from thence to be drawn upon a hurdle through the midst of the City, and so to the place of execution, there to be hanged by the neck and taken down alive—your bodies to be opened, and your bowels taken out and burned before your face; your bodies to be quartered—your heads and quarters to be disposed of, and so God have mercy on your souls."

In the face of this horrendous sentence, our young Earl spoke in his gentle voice: "I do submit myself to death, yet not despairing of Her Majesty's mercy; for I know she is merciful, and if she please to extend her mercy to me, I shall with all humility receive it." Many of those present were deeply moved, and one spectator wrote that the young Earl's "sweet temper did breed most compassionate affections in all men."

The grotesque punishment was carried out on some of the conspirators, but the Queen later agreed to a private beheading for both Essex and Southampton. The date of 25 February was set for Essex, with that of Southampton to follow soon after.

Then the Queen had her personal revenge on Will and his company. They were given a royal command to perform at the Court the play *King Richard II* on the evening before the execution of Essex.

When he returned that night, Will told me bitterly, "She knew exactly what she was doing. At every speech about Bolingbroke's popularity, she gave an evil smile and muttered remarks about 'Devereaux,' as she called Essex. She gloated over us as we were forced to play the scene deposing the King. And when it was over, she sent for me to come to her. As I knelt before her, she gave me a sharp look and said, 'Devereaux was a devil, but your friend is not.' Then she winked one eye and waved me away."

The next morning, Robert Devereaux, the Earl of Essex, at the age of thirty-five, was beheaded. Later that day came the word, to our great joy, that Southampton's sentence had been commuted to life imprisonment.

Prison for life may not sound like a great prospect, but who knew what changes might take place in the future? At least, while he was still alive, there was always hope.

Chapter 4

MURDER

i

After the devastating failure of the Essex rebellion, I was glad to be back in Stratford. Rosanna and I had begun to realize that our children were growing up. My Susanna and her Agnes were attractive young ladies of eighteen, and her son David, now sixteen, was away at Magdalen College at Oxford. My Judith, also sixteen, missed David, her loyal companion, and was delighted when he wrote to invite her to attend a ball at his college. And of course, he had added, his sister and Susanna must come too.

And so it was that on a cool spring day, Rosanna and I set out with all three of our girls for Oxford, some forty miles from Stratford. With its many colleges forming the famous University, as well as its prominence as a trading center, Oxford was a popular destination for people all over the country. Until now, we had merely passed through the town on the way to London, so I looked forward to spending some time there and seeing the sights.

The road from Stratford was well-traveled and was seldom attacked by robbers, and since I had never encountered any trouble after my first journey to London, I had put that worry aside.

Early in the morning of the day we departed, a large party of people had gathered at the Swan Inn, roughly forming a line of riders two or three abreast. We had agreed to go pillion style, with Judith riding behind Susanna, and Agnes riding behind her mother, leaving me to start on a single saddle, with plans to change off many times during the day. The boxes containing all our finery went by pack-horse.

The weather was variable. During the course of the long day, it rained once or twice, and we pulled the hoods of our cloaks over our heads until the skies cleared again. On the whole, it was a cheerful crowd, and the hours passed pleasantly. Many of us were acquaintances in the town, and there was much moving up and down the line as people chatted with friends.

At midday, we stopped at a tavern for a meal and changes of horse for those who needed them. By late afternoon, Rosanna and I were feeling weary, but the girls were much too excited to think about fatigue. Darkness had fallen when at last we arrived at the inn not far from Magdalen College, where rooms had been reserved for us.

We were at supper when David arrived, glowing with pride at having us there. He was still young enough to hug each of us in turn, although I guessed that if some of his classmates had been present, he might have been more restrained.

The next day, David showed us through his own college. Then we walked through the town, visited some of the other colleges, and were taken in punts along the river, enjoying the beauty of the old buildings, some dating from three centuries or more in the past.

Then came the hour to dress for the ball. Susanna and Agnes had already attended dancing parties in our own vicinity, but this was Judith's first ball and her first long gown. The rose-colored fabric of fine gauze, over a silk petticoat, set off her dark eyes and deep brown hair, and her shapely figure added to her charm.

When David came to call for us, he looked at Judith with admiring eyes, and when he held out his arm to escort his mother, Rosanna smiled and said, "You may take Judith, my dear. I shall come with Anne."

As Rosanna and I sat with the chaperones, watching the young people, I had to push down the pain of imagining my brilliant and lively Hamnet there, at the same age as Rosanna's David, a student at Magdalen, attending his first college ball. However, four years of practice had enabled me to close off those thoughts and focus on the present.

We smiled as David danced the first quadrille with Judith, and the glow on both their faces was sweet to see. When they weren't dancing, they were sitting in rapt conversation, and when some of David's young friends came to ask Judith for a dance, she demurely danced with one or two but came back to David. Rosanna and I watched in mild astonishment as these two, who had grown up like brother and sister, began to look at each other in a new light.

Rosanna spoke fondly of her first balls, when she had gone to London to stay with old friends of her father's family and had met her first husband there. Watching the young people dance, I knew she was seeing a reflection of her own romance, and remembering the brief years of happiness before her husband was taken from her.

For my part, the whole scene reminded me that I had never gone to a ball like this in my youth. There had been a few rural parties with dancing, but at seventeen, I had gone to stay with Stephen Brent, and my life had taken a different turn.

Did I regret having missed all this? Not on your life. I seldom thought of Stephen, but I knew I wouldn't have traded those years of his warmth and affection for all the fine gowns and romantic evenings in the world.

David had made a point of presenting some of the upperclassmen to Agnes and Susanna, knowing that they would find his own first-year friends too young for their notice. The girls made an attractive contrast, Agnes with the striking Italian coloring of her mother, and Susanna fair like both Will and me, with what I saw as Will's lively charm.

Both girls danced for a time, then sat with us to rest.

After a time, they were approached by two young Dons, head tutors of the college who were keeping an eye on the younger undergraduates. Both men were in their early twenties, I guessed. Each couple danced once, then sat talking, and presently, all four were sitting at a table together in eager conversation, seeming to forget the dancing altogether.

After some time, the girls brought the young men to meet us, and Susanna's companion said to me, "These young ladies are better informed than most of our young chaps. It seems a pity that young women cannot attend University."

I smiled. "Perhaps it will happen some day." But neither of us really believed that for a moment.

During the years after our formal lessons to the girls, they had continued to read widely on all sorts of subjects, and it was gratifying to see that their eager minds were appreciated by these intelligent young men.

Back in Stratford, all the pleasures of the visit to Oxford were talked over for days, until life went back, as it always does, to its everyday routines.

Young Tom Quiney still helped out the sexton of the church, although Richard often laughed at the pittance he earned. Being Richard, he never understood his son's need for being a servant of his faith. What surprised me was that, although Richard was often openly impatient with Tom, he always stopped short of being actually harsh to him. The fact that Tom still lived with his grandfather Adrian probably kept them free of daily irritations, and Tom seemed to be unaware of Richard's lack of affection, beaming with pleasure at the slightest sign of approval from his father.

We now noticed that Nate Fletcher had begun to take an interest in Tom. The past years had been a tragic time for Nate and his beloved niece Libby. When she married, I had seen her glowing with happiness, but fate had not been kind to Libby. Her invalid mother died, and in the following year, Libby's only child, a little daughter, died in infancy. Now, only seven years after her wedding, her young husband was killed in an accident. Her grandmother, Rebecca, still lived, but was frail and not clear in her mind.

Nate had tried to help Libby in any way he could over the years, but now he felt utterly helpless. "I can't seem to do aught for her," he would say to me, his voice shaking. "She doesn't need money. Jeb left her well provided for. She doesn't complain. She doesn't even weep any more. She just seems to be frozen up, like."

And he would ask me over again, "What shall I do?"

I knew what he meant, for I sometimes saw Libby in the high street, walking slowly, as if she were in a dream. Her features were still as pretty as when she was a girl, but there was no life in her face. One day I invited her to come home with me and have something to eat, but she smiled vaguely, shook her head, and walked on.

Nate said many people had tried to help her, but no one

could get a response, and I had never known her well enough to feel that I could do what others could not.

Perhaps it was his distress over Libby that kindled Nate's interest in Tom Quiney. "He is a serious boy," he told me, "and he is always well-behaved. I like that."

That seemed to be Nate's criterion for paternal approval, I thought, remembering his pride in his little Libby who was "good as gold" and "never gave a mite of trouble."

Soon Nate had brought Tom to visit Libby and was pleased that she seemed to like the boy, letting him sit and chatter to her, although she seldom made any response.

Nate sometimes invited Tom to spend a few days with him at his farm, excursions which the boy enjoyed. Whatever he lacked in intellectual interests, Tom was fascinated by farming life, eagerly learning about the rotation of crops, the care of the livestock, and the ways in which the changes in weather affected the farmer's fortunes.

Soon Tom was calling him Uncle Nate. Telling me about all this, Tom would say, "That's what I would like to do. When I'm of age, I believe I will buy a farm and learn from Uncle Nate what I need to know."

I didn't ask him where the money might come from to realize this dream. I couldn't see Richard forking over any substantial sum for the boy. Money seemed to run through Richard's fingers like water.

But when later Tom repeated his resolve to buy a farm, I did ask him if he thought Richard would do this for him.

"Oh, Papa? No, that won't be necessary. I mean to buy it with my own money!"

That was how I learned something that none of us had known before. Tom's grandparents in Windermere had left him a sizeable sum of money.

"I am so glad to have a plan, at last," he said eagerly.

"Of course, I shall give a sum to the church, but until now I had no idea what I wanted to do with my life. Now I do."

"Have you talked with your father about this, Tom?"

"No, not now. I don't think he would be interested in farming, do you?"

I smiled and agreed.

"But you see," he went on, "it won't matter. When I am twenty-one, I will have my own money. And it won't be long to wait. I am already nineteen, and in two years, I shall be ready. Uncle Nate will advise me about it then."

I was pleased that Tom had found a surrogate uncle. Nate seldom showed the bursts of anger he used to engage in, although the tragedies that occurred to his Libby had brought forth some violent wailings against the unfairness of life. On the whole, he had grown calmer with the passage of time.

Now Rosanna confessed to me that she had a new worry. Her brother Edward was in desperate financial straits. During the trials for treason, he had been convicted as one of the conspirators and was extremely lucky to escape with a heavy fine, rather than with imprisonment or worse. Now, on top of the huge sums he had contributed to the Essex camp before the coup, he suddenly found himself close to bankruptcy.

"I don't know what to do, Anne," Rosanna said. "Edward has lent large sums of money to Richard, and now he needs to have the money. Richard is insisting that I repay his debts, but the amounts are very large, and I don't want to rob David of his inheritance from his father."

I saw her problem, and it was soon clear that the great friendship between Richard and Edward was at an end. Edward saw his sister only when her husband was not at home, and one evening at our house, when Richard appeared, Edward sniffed and pointedly walked out of the house.

When Will came home soon afterward, we heard some startling news from Edward. We had assumed that his rift with Richard Quiney was over the money, but we soon learned it was something much worse than that. Will and I were sitting in the garden one afternoon when Edward appeared and announced that he must talk to someone or he would go mad.

Will raised an eyebrow and pointed to a stone bench near by.

"Sit down and tell us what you mean."

Edward began in a sort of hoarse whisper. "I'm afraid I may have done something quite dreadful."

Assuming he was dramatizing as usual, I said, "I'm sure that can't be true, Edward."

"But I may have been responsible for the failure of the rebellion!"

Running out of patience, Will snapped, "And what makes you think that?"

His voice trembling, Edward whispered, "It's been nearly two months since that dreadful night, and I can't sleep for thinking about it. You see, it's Richard. I believe he betrayed our cause!"

"How could he have done that, Edward?"

"You remember, Will, the day your company did the special performance of *King Richard II*, the one we paid extra money for?"

Will scowled. "I'm not likely to forget that."

"Yes. Well, Richard was there and came with me when we went back to Essex House. That evening, there was a meeting with those of us who were the most trusted advisors, and the secret plan was laid to lead our troops the next morning to St. Paul's Churchyard for Lord Essex to address the people and enlist their support. Secrecy was vital, as rumor had it that the Court was deploying its forces in the opposite direction.

"Well, after the meeting, Richard was waiting for me in the crowded courtyard, and I told him about the plan."

"*You told Richard?* Why on earth did you do that?"

Edward flushed. "He was my friend and I believed I could trust him. But an hour later, when I looked everywhere for him, he had slipped away. Then, in the morning, we learned that our plan was known and the streets were blocked."

"Have you asked Richard about this?"

"Of course. He denies it, but instead of being outraged, he looks sly. And then, he had a purse of money the next day. I asked him where it came from, and he said someone had paid off a debt. But I don't know if I can believe him. You see, Will?"

Will was furious. "That swine Quiney. If he did this, I tell you, Edward, hanging is too good for him. I'd like to have him at my mercy. I'd cheerfully run him through with my sword!"

I asked, "But Edward, why didn't you say something before now?"

"I was afraid I would be blamed if it was true."

Will snarled. "Damned right you would. How could you be such a fool as to tell Quiney anything?"

Poor Edward was weeping by now. "What shall I do?" he wailed.

Will said, "It's no good doing anything now."

Privately I wondered if Richard's action, if true, could have been the deciding factor that night. I suspected that the rebellion was ill-fated from the beginning and that the Queen's forces would have defeated the Earls, if not that night, then soon enough. However, I certainly didn't express this to Will, and besides, it didn't alter the suspicion that Richard had betrayed his friends, whether successfully or not.

Now Will told Edward it might be wise for him to go abroad for awhile until matters had cooled.

I said, "Why not go and visit your cousin Carla and the Count?"

This seemingly innocent remark set poor Edward off again. His lips trembled, and his voice shook. "You must promise never to tell anyone, but the Count was a member of a secret conspiracy that supported the rebellion. He gave huge sums and now he is desperate to recover his losses. He wanted money from me, if you can imagine, just when I am stripped to the bone!"

When Edward had gone, I expressed my surprise that the Count had been involved in the conspiracy. I knew there had always been powerful Catholic families on the Continent who would be glad to see the last of the Protestant Queen, but I didn't know Carla's husband was actively allied with them. I said, "I wonder if Edward was the one who drew the Count into it."

Will shook his head. "Who knows? It might have been the other way about. The Earls of Southampton have always been closely allied with Catholic families abroad. Maybe Antonio has been a long-time ally and lured Edward into the whole thing."

I agreed. Edward was easily swayed, and the vigorous and dynamic Count was more likely to have been the leader.

Soon after Will had gone back to London, Rosanna came to me in tears. "I gave in to Richard, Anne, and paid his debts to Edward, and I have had to use money that truly belongs to David's inheritance."

"But Rosanna dear, couldn't you simply have refused?"

Her face flushed, and she shook her head. "He was so very—that is, he made it very difficult—" And her voice broke in a sob.

I sensed she was holding something back, but I felt I could do nothing except to murmur my concern and hope things would mend.

But what Rosanna wouldn't tell me didn't stop the children. David was home on a holiday, and all four of them came to me a few hours later, in my upstairs sitting-room.

Susanna, her face flushed, began. "We have decided we must talk to you, Mama."

The others nodded, and Agnes said, "Something terrible just happened. Uncle Richard was very angry with Mama and was shouting at her, and I rushed into the room, although I'd been told to stay away, and I saw him strike her!"

"And that's not the worst," cried Judith. "Tell her all of it."

Agnes's dark eyes blazed. "I ran up to Uncle Richard and tried to hit at him, and I shouted, 'How could you do this to my mother?' "

Agnes paused, her breath coming in gasps, then went on. "And he swung his hand against the side of my head and knocked me to the floor! And I got up and ran for David."

The boy sat with his fists curled. David was a fine lad but slight in build, and not a match for a man the size of Richard.

"I went for him," he said, "and managed a blow to his chin, when all of a sudden, before I could hit again, he pushed me away and fell on his knees in front of Mama and started weeping and saying he was sorry and he didn't know what came over him, and could she ever forgive him, and it would never happen again, and so on."

Now Judith spoke up proudly. "David was so brave to try to attack him, but what could he do?"

All the eager faces turned to me for help, and I sat for a moment, thinking. What could they do? For that matter, what could anyone do, unless Rosanna was willing to leave Richard? Such a solution was not unheard of, but it was very difficult for a woman to live separately from her husband, no matter what the cause.

I was furious with Richard, but I didn't see what the young people could do to help matters. All I could give them was sympathy. I cautioned them to say nothing to anyone else, as it would cause their mother embarrassment and would not help to heal matters.

Agnes said, "I know Mama. She's so kind, she will probably forgive him. But I won't. *I hate him!* He pretends to love my mother, but it's all false. He only wants her money."

The next day, I reported this to George Camden, and I was astonished at the violent anger that burst from that usually calm and sensible man.

"I promise you, Anne," he growled. "If this happens again, he'll have to answer to me! Legally, there's nothing I can do. A husband has control over his wife's money, and he can exercise what the law calls 'discipline' as he sees fit. But, I'll tell you this: He had better not try it again. I'll do anything to protect Rosanna."

I looked at George and saw something I ought to have seen before. "You care for Rosanna, don't you?"

His round face still flushed, he muttered, "Always have, I suppose."

Fond as I was of him, I couldn't keep the irritation out of my voice. "My dear man, why have you never . . . ?"

"I suppose I didn't think she would look at me. She's so lovely, and I thought some fine-looking chap would come along for her. I never thought it would be Quiney!"

I wanted to say, "Why didn't you at least try?" But when George had gone, I thought how sure we are that we could manage other people's lives for them, but do we do any better with our own? How do I know how Rosanna would have responded to George? And if she had refused him, it would have been devastating to him.

I soon learned from the girls that indeed Rosanna had forgiven Richard and believed his promise that he would never behave that way again. She never mentioned it to me, and I ground my teeth in silence.

After the ball at David's college at Oxford, I had wondered if Susanna and Agnes would hear again from the young Dons who had spent so much time dancing and talking with them. Indeed, a letter came for Agnes, who was delighted to hear from her admirer and replied at once. A letter also came for Susanna, but she sent a polite reply, with no encouragement to continue the correspondence.

A new doctor had come to Stratford. The first time Doctor John Hall came to the house to attend to Mary, Susanna had met him, chatted with him, and from that day, never looked back. "That is the kind of man I should like to marry," she had said to me. And I agreed.

Susanna had never cared for mere boys, and Dr. Hall was six years her senior. He was intelligent, thoughtful, and good-looking. Susanna was not as impulsive as her father, but like him, when she saw what she wanted, she generally got it. And she wanted Dr. Hall. Fortunately, he was as smitten as she, but he moved cautiously. He spoke to me of having to establish his practice before taking any "step" for the future, and I smiled quietly and agreed.

Susanna was in no hurry. "I know he loves me, Mama," she said, "and that's all that matters. I can wait."

David went back to his college, and the girls were soon distracted by the news that their Italian cousin was coming for a visit. It had been nine years since Carla and the Count had come to Stratford, and once meanwhile Rosanna had taken her children to Siena, where they had evidently had a grand time.

I remembered hearing about the visit when they returned. Agnes, aged fourteen at the time, had told us, "Aunt Carla is the same as she's always been. All she thinks about is going to balls and wearing her fine clothes, but she was very sweet to us all the same. Of course, we like the Count. He is so handsome, even though he is *old,* and he gives her lovely jewels." And David had laughed scornfully. "He calls her his 'piccolo tesoro'—his little treasure."

Although the children thought Carla silly, they were nevertheless fond of their aunt and were disappointed when the visit was postponed. It seemed that the Count was delayed by some troubling matters regarding his estate, and they would come later on. After what Edward had told us, I could guess what the "troubling matters" were. I said nothing to anyone, not even to George, but I figured the Count's wife wouldn't be getting any expensive jewels for awhile.

ii

Some months had passed when we got the exciting news from Will that his company was going on tour and would stop in Stratford in the month of July. The notices went up all around town that they would be performing Will's play *Julius Caesar*, which had been a great favorite in London.

One day, about that time, Tom Quiney came to me in deep distress. He had gone to Libby's house that day to bring her some flowers from the churchyard. It was market day, and Tom had seen Libby's maidservant there doing the weekly shopping. Finding Libby's door unlatched, he had come in quietly, expecting to find her sitting motionless in her chair as usual. Hearing sounds from another room, Tom had peered in and seen Libby and his father lying on a bed with their arms entwined, making little murmuring sounds. He had dropped the flowers on a chair and fled from the house.

Tom was frantic with fear and grief. "He will surely go to hell and damnation if he doesn't repent, won't he? He's committing *fornication*," he cried, stumbling over the word. "And not only that, Papa is married, so it is *adultery* too, isn't it?"

I noticed he wasn't worried about Libby's immortal soul, only that of his beloved father.

I soothed him as best I could, assuring him that it would all come right in the end but cautioning him against saying a single word about it to his father, or for that matter, to anyone else. At last he gave me his solemn promise.

As the time approached for Will's company to arrive in town, Rosanna learned that Carla and the Count were due to come for their promised visit and would be there in time for the play. As luck would have it, the Count was again delayed, and this time his wife came on ahead.

At the first of our evening parties, Richard was giving Carla the full treatment of his charm, and Rosanna seemed glad that her Richard was being cordial to her beloved cousin. I decided to keep a sharp eye on the two of them but saw nothing alarming. I did notice, though, that as the days passed, Carla's face had a rosy glow and she was all smiles. I was aware that Carla had been given a bedroom and boudoir on the top floor of Rosanna's large house, and who knew what nocturnal visits Richard might make? And I soon learned that my guess wasn't far wrong.

It was a few days before the Count was expected to arrive when Susanna and Agnes came to me, more distressed than ever before. Agnes had been sent upstairs to Carla's room to fetch something, and going into the boudoir, she could hear voices in the adjacent bedroom.

"It was Uncle Richard, and they were making love, I *know* they were! I dropped something on the floor so they would know someone was there, and their voices stopped at once. I'm sure one of them opened the door enough to see me as I went down the stairs."

"What did you do, Agnes?" I asked.

"I went straight down to Mama and told her what I had heard, and you know Mama. She said I must have been mistaken, and not to think about it again. What shall I do now?"

I said gently, "If your dear Mama does not want to believe it, there is really nothing anyone can do."

The girls reluctantly agreed, Agnes saying over and over, *"I hate him! I hate him!"*

It was the only thing I could have said to Agnes, but I seethed with anger myself to learn that what I had feared had indeed happened.

The next day, whatever the cause, we all noticed a marked change in Carla. Her cheeks were pale, her eyes dull, and her mouth sullen. No one seeing her now would consider her beautiful, I thought. Rosanna was concerned that her dear cousin might be ill, but I didn't waste any time worrying about Carla.

Within a few days, Will and his company arrived, and the preparations were in full swing. The play would be given at the Guild Hall, where the company had performed *A Midsummer Night's Dream* so many years ago. Will had suggested that we have the reception at our house instead of at the inn.

The Count arrived in time for the play, and when he came, all of Carla's sulks cleared away and she was full of smiles. The Count was charming to all of us, and Will, who hadn't been at home on their previous visit, was favorably impressed when they met. Rosanna proudly presented Will to her cousin, and Carla gave a deep curtsey and said it was a great honor to meet the illustrious Master Shakespeare. I saw Will look into her face and bow with a kind of mock humility that amused me. I knew he had heard enough about Carla not to take her seriously.

After the disaster with *King Richard II*, Will had sworn off any further excursions into English history. He had turned now to Plutarch's *Lives of the Noble Grecians and Romans* for his source for the new play. If there were any political implications in the story of Julius Caesar, the message could only be that betraying and killing popular monarchs didn't pay in the end but simply led to a cycle of more betrayal and disaster. Nothing the Queen could object to, I thought with relief.

In the years since the company had come to Stratford, Will's fame had grown, and the audience that thronged the Guild Hall knew that their local son of Warwickshire was acclaimed throughout the realm.

Will played the role of Caesar himself. "It's the shortest role in the play," he told me with a laugh. "Caesar is dead at the beginning of the third act."

Will's position in the company was now such that he

could act more or less when he wanted to and often passed up the acting to devote more time to playwriting, or taking minor roles to save time and effort.

Now, as the play began, the Stratford spectators were gripped with suspense, and breathless when the conspirators surrounded the great Caesar at the Capitol, each one taking out his sword to stab him, so that all were equally guilty. They groaned when Caesar sees Brutus among them and cries out, *"Et tu, Brute?"* at the betrayal of his friend. They gave a collective great sigh as he fell.

But we had not quite seen the last of Will, for civil war had followed the death of Caesar, and on the eve of battle, when Brutus is still deeply troubled by his role in the treachery, he is visited by the ghost of Caesar, warning Brutus of ultimate defeat.

When Will appeared, draped in a thin white cloth to give a ghost-like image of a shroud, I heard a gasp and saw Carla clutch her husband's hand, her face pale and twisted in fear. The costume would deceive nobody, but to Carla, with her obsession with the occult, the image must have been frightening. How can she be so silly, I thought, but I saw the Count pat her hand and murmur soothingly to her.

At the end of the play, the Hall rang with shouts and stamping of feet in praise of the performance.

The reception at our house for the members of the company and our personal friends began with such lively spirits that the last thing anyone could have imagined was that it would end in tragedy.

I often wondered afterward if we should have seen the murder coming. Richard had antagonized plenty of people, but would we have expected that anyone would actually kill him? And certainly not at a social gathering like this one.

The weather had held, and in the dusky light, the guests

roamed about the rooms and strolled in the garden. Young David Wilson's long vacation had begun, and he was accompanied by Charles Grey, the young Don who had admired Agnes at the college ball and was now in regular correspondence with her. The two were delighted to meet again, and joined with Susanna and her Doctor Hall in a congenial foursome.

George Camden was there, looking younger than his fifty years, and making me impatient, thinking that he might have married Rosanna long ago if he had had more gumption. Edward had come in honor of the Count, but I noticed he avoided speaking to Richard.

Carla was dazzling in a scarlet gown that clung to her bosom, its long sleeves gorgeously embroidered in gold. Her dark hair, piled high, held a tiara that glittered with diamonds, and her beautiful eyes glowed as she received admiring glances. I noticed she was all smiles now, with no apparent effect from her fright over the ghost of Caesar. The actors, including Will, remained in their handsome costumes, and everyone partook liberally of the food and drink I had provided.

I was pleased to see that Richard was being markedly attentive to his wife and clearly avoiding Carla.

At one point in the evening, I saw Carla approach Will and appear to ask him a question. He nodded and walked through the entrance hall to an anteroom where guests deposited their cloaks and outer clothing. I was about to turn away when I saw Carla following him. What is she up to now? I thought, and I sauntered along at a distance behind her. Then I stepped across the corridor to a doorway where I could observe them without being seen. I couldn't hear what was said, but what happened was exactly what I expected. Carla was standing close to Will, putting her arms up toward him and giving him her best flirtatious looks. I saw him take hold of her wrists and put her hands down at her sides. Their voices murmured, and I could see her trying again, as if she could not believe he would refuse her. Then I saw Will emerge, looking extremely irritated. Minutes later, Carla came out, flushed and angry. She didn't lose any time, I thought. She'll probably try again if she has the chance.

I went back into the large parlor where I saw a group gathered around some object that old John was holding up.

"It belonged to my grandfather," John was saying, and I saw that it was the jeweled dagger that was kept in a glass cabinet against the wall. John was chuckling, "I'm glad no one had this in his hand when they were stabbing Will in the play. Look here, how sharp it is." John removed the leather sheath and several men touched the blade gingerly.

Nate Fletcher, sitting stiffly beside John, frowned and put out his hand to hold the dagger. "Watch out, Nate," someone called out. "You don't want to lose your temper when you're holding that thing!"

Scowling, Nate said nothing but handed it to young Tom Quiney, who drew back and didn't touch it.

John grinned and took it back. "It won't bite, Tom," he said, and Tom flushed in embarrassment.

David Wilson, who had seen it many times in the case but had never touched it, now put out his hand. "Please, sir, may I show it to my friends?"

John, who was fond of the boy, put it back in the sheath, saying, "Of course you may." I went off to check on the food supplies and forgot about the dagger.

Some of the musicians had brought their instruments and generously played for us, and when they played some of the songs from Will's plays that had become popularly known, people gathered round them in the salon and joined in the singing.

In the warm evening, many people strolled in the cool of the garden, where we had placed torches here and there to give a faint light along the paths. Others sat in chairs along the terrace, or came in to take refreshments and to join with friends in the ground-floor reception rooms.

Some time after the church bells had tolled the hour of ten, the members of the company began to take their leave. When the actors had gone, and darkness had fallen at last, I was beginning to think it was time for the rest to do likewise, but no one had made a move as yet. I had noticed Will going out to the garden, and when the bells tolled eleven hours, I wondered at his not coming back in.

Some time later, I was standing on the terrace when I heard a shout and saw the Count emerging from the garden path to my left. At almost the same moment, Will appeared, strolling slowly along the path at my right. The Count was calling, "Someone is hurt! Send help!"

Then Will began to run, calling, "Get Timothy, Anne." And he crossed the terrace and turned to follow as the Count went back down the path. I gave the order to send Timothy, our head manservant, and to bring torches, and I hurried after Will and the Count. As we stumbled and lurched in the darkness, Will asked Antonio if he knew who it was, and I heard him say, "Yes, it is Richard, and I believe he is dead."

When we finally reached the far corner of the garden under the elm tree, I could see the body of a man lying face down on the ground. Will lifted the man's head. "Yes, it's Richard," he said. And there was no doubt that he was dead.

The Count bent over and picked up an object from the

ground near the body. Even in the darkness, the flash of the jewels was visible on the handle of old John's dagger, and when the torches came, we could all see the huge patch of blood on the back of Richard's coat. The Count carefully slid the dagger back into the sheath that lay nearby, and they looked around the area for other signs that might relate to what was obviously a murder.

"I'll tell Rosanna," I said, and headed for the house.

I found the three girls standing with Rosanna and Carla on the terrace. I took them into the house, sat down beside Rosanna, took her hand in mine, and told her what had happened. The girls clustered round Rosanna, who was shocked but dry-eyed, while Carla covered her face with her hands and gave muffled shrieks. I hope she doesn't decide on hysterics, I thought, but when Carla saw that no one was noticing her, she wiped her eyes with a frilly lace handkerchief and merely sniffled.

Presently we heard the men coming, carrying the body of Richard Quiney on a litter. "In here," I heard Will say. The servants quickly cleared the large table in the room where we had our meals, and they laid the body there. The Count went off in search of his wife, and Will sent one of the servants to summon the Sheriff. Then he noticed something in the dead man's hand, and opened his fingers to reveal a gold coin of considerable value, handing it to George Camden for safekeeping.

iii

Everyone now gathered in the large parlor, where Will said, "I've sent for Sheriff Hodge. The gate in the back wall was open, and someone must have come in that way. He should be apprehended before he can get away."

The Sheriff came, accompanied by two of his men. He was told how Richard's body had been found, and when he learned about the open garden gate, he sent the men off at once to look for any suspicious persons in the neighborhood.

Now he took out a sheaf of paper and a pencil and cleared his throat. He looked around the room as we all sat in a kind of rough circle, stunned into silence by the shock of Richard's death. The Sheriff went round the room, asking each of us our whereabouts during the evening and when we had last seen Richard.

He began with Mary at his right, who looked dazed and confused. "Dear Richard," she murmured. "He was here in the parlor sometimes during the evening, but I never went into the garden, did I, John?"

He pressed her hand. "No, of course not, my dear. No one suspects you."

Mary's voice quavered. "Poor Richard. How dreadful! Adrian's gone home. Someone must tell him." John assured her that he had already sent one of the servants to do that, and suggested that she must go to bed now. The Sheriff nodded, and her maid was summoned to take her upstairs.

Then John told Hodge that he blamed himself, as he should never have taken the dagger out of the case, and everyone tried to assure him it was not his fault. When asked, he said he had gone into the garden earlier in the evening but had sat with Mary the last hour or so and had no recollection of when he last saw Richard. "He came in and out a few times, but I can't say exactly when."

The Sheriff wrote laboriously on his paper, then looking around the circle, he turned to David. "Master Wilson, we have heard that you took t' dagger to show it to your friend. Did you return t' dagger to t' case?"

David frowned. "I meant to do that, but I remember handing it to my Uncle Edward while we were in the library, and then I'm afraid I forgot about it."

"And when did you see your father last?"

David flushed. "He's not my father, but to answer your question, I saw him sitting with my mother in the parlor for a time, but I don't remember seeing him after that time at all. I walked in the garden with Miss Judith for a bit. Then we came in and had refreshments with my sister and our friends."

The Sheriff knew all of us who lived in Stratford, at least by sight, but now he turned to David's young friend, who was a stranger.

"May I ask your name, sir?"

"My name is Charles Grey. I am a Don at Magdalen College at Oxford. I saw the dagger when young David Wilson brought it into the library. I touched the blade but I don't remember seeing it afterward."

"And what was your acquaintance with Master Quiney, the gentleman as is deceased, sir?"

Charles replied that he had not met the gentleman until that very evening, as the stepfather of his friend David Wilson and David's sister, Miss Agnes. With an engaging smile, he admitted to having spent most of the evening with his young friends and did not notice the whereabouts of the parents.

Agnes was next, and all her resentment of Richard poured out as she stood and faced the Sheriff. "I did not notice anything about my stepfather. I disliked him and I had no interest in where he was or what he was doing."

Hodge showed no response, but doggedly wrote his

notes. Then he looked up at Agnes and asked, in a flat tone, "And did you go into the garden during the evening, Miss Agnes?"

"Yes, several of us walked together in the garden, but I did not go alone, and I did not kill him."

Rosanna gasped but said not a word.

Judith confirmed what the others had said, adding boldly that Richard was "not a good person."

Susanna came next. "I do remember seeing Richard on the terrace. I noticed that all of the players in my father's company had gone, and I wondered if others would be going too, so it must have been a little before eleven, because soon afterward I heard the bells begin, and when I looked out again, Richard was not there."

"And what was Master Richard doing at t' time you saw him, Miss Susanna?"

"He was standing there, looking out into the garden. He was frowning and looking rather angry, but I didn't really care if he was disturbed about something. He is—was—a very wicked person."

Hodge appeared to take no notice of this remark, but stolidly continued to write.

Now he turned to Edward. "Master Bushell, we have heard that your nephew handed t' dagger to you?"

All eyes turned to Edward, who looked startled. "Yes, indeed, he did, and I believe the young ladies were there as well as the young gentlemen. Then the young people all left the room, and, oh, dear, let me see, yes, I laid the dagger on the table by the window. I am sure that's what I did."

The sheriff asked, "Was it in t' sheath at that time, sir?"

Edward looked startled. "In the sheath? Oh, yes, it must have been, must it not? I should not have handled it otherwise. But I did not see it again after that. Of course, I ought to have returned it to the cabinet where it is usually kept, and oh, dear, I do wish I had done so, but of course, how could one know that someone—I mean, that is to say, how could one know what would happen?"

Asked when he had last seen Richard, Edward said he remembered thinking it was growing late and perhaps time to be taking his leave, when he saw Richard on the terrace.

"You and he was friendly like, was you not, sir?" Everybody in town, I thought, knew that, even the Sheriff.

Edward's lips tightened. "Not just at present, no."

"What time was it as you saw t' gentleman, sir?"

"It must have been close on eleven. He was standing on the terrace, just as Miss Susanna said, and it seemed to be soon after that I heard the bells and noticed Richard was no longer there."

Now poor Hodge fumbled with his pencil and looked at Rosanna, addressing her first as "Mistress Wilson," then apologetically correcting it to "Mistress Quiney." In his homely way he expressed his sympathy for her loss and asked if she recalled when she last saw her husband.

Rosanna showed no sign of tears, and her voice was low but perfectly steady. "He was here with me off and on during the evening. Then I went upstairs for a bit. For a time, I was standing at the drawing-room window, looking out at the garden."

"Did you see anyone at that time, madam?"

Her voice unchanged, Rosanna said, "I suppose there were people standing about but I didn't notice. Then I turned away and came down here to the parlor. It was then that I heard the bells toll for eleven."

"And did you see your husband again, after that?"

The question that would have brought most widows to instant tears had no such effect on Rosanna. She showed no emotion, and her voice was cold as she said, "No, I did not."

Hodge asked her then if she wished to retire, but she refused. "I am quite all right, thank you. I shall remain here."

Hodge nodded and turned to Nate Fletcher, asking when he saw Richard last.

Nate sat bolt upright, stiff as a poker. Now that I thought about it, he had looked like that all evening. Whether sitting or walking about, he had never seemed to speak to anyone.

Now, he looked at the Sheriff and tried to speak, but no sound came. He tried to clear his throat, to no avail. Someone handed him a glass of ale, and he seized it and drank it all in rapid gulps.

That seemed to do the trick, for a hoarse whisper came from his throat. "I saw him in the garden."

"About what time was that, sir?"

"Time? I don't know about time."

"Do you remember hearing t' bells ring at eleven hours, sir?"

His face rigid, Nate stared at Hodge. "Richard's dead," he said. "He's dead."

"Yes, sir, we know that. Now we want to learn who killed him."

"Who killed him?" Nate shook his head, and when asked again, said nothing more.

"Is there anything you can tell us, sir?" Hodge asked, obviously without hope of getting more out of Nate.

He gave up and turned to Tom, expressing sympathy for the loss of his father.

Tom looked absolutely stricken. His face was chalk white and traces of tears streaked his cheeks. "I can't believe it! I never thought anyone would—that is, I can't believe that all this happened."

Asked when he last saw his father, he seemed bewildered. "I don't know just when I saw him last. He was in the parlor sometimes, and he was on the terrace, but I don't remember what time it was at all."

Hodge thanked the young man, repeating his condolences, and then turned to George. "Master Camden, you know the law. Would there be other questions as I ought to ask?"

George said he had done admirably so far, and added that as for himself, he had definitely seen Richard going into the garden earlier in the evening, but did not recall seeing him afterward other than here in the parlor, where George had remained. Certainly he had not seen him after the hour of eleven.

At my turn, I had nothing to add. The fact is, I had kept a sharp eye on Richard for awhile, noticing that he stuck close to Rosanna and seemed to avoid Carla. I simply told the Sheriff that I had been occupied and had no idea where Richard was when the bells tolled.

Now at last it was Will's turn, and we were all surprised to learn that he was the only one who seemed to have any significant information. He had been in the opposite corner of the garden under the linden tree shortly before the bells tolled for eleven, and had seen Richard just at that time!

"I was sitting on the bench near the back gate," he said, "talking with a gentleman, when Richard came hurrying past us. I spoke to him and he seemed startled. He muttered some reply and strode on along the path at the back of the garden that leads to the opposite corner, where his body was later found under the elm tree. It was perhaps three or four minutes after that that the bells tolled for eleven."

"Who is this gentleman, sir?"

"I don't know. He was a stranger. He said he was just passing through the town."

"Can you describe him?"

"Yes. He was elderly, and he wore a long gray cloak. His hair was white. He was courteous and well-spoken."

The Sheriff asked if anyone else in the party had seen this gentleman, and met only with negative responses.

Now he turned back to Will, asking him to continue. Will said he had stayed chatting with the gentleman for some time. Then, as he was strolling back toward the house, he heard the Count's voice calling and rushed out to learn what had happened.

The Sheriff now addressed the Count. "I believe, sir, as you was t' one as found t' body of t' deceased gentleman?"

Everyone leaned forward eagerly to hear what the Count had to say. With his distinguished head and aristocratic bearing, he looked the image of a noble Roman in Will's play. His voice was resonant, as he answered the question. "Yes, Sheriff, it was I. The bells have tolled for eleven hours, and some time has passed, when I walk into the garden. I am looking for my wife, who I think might be strolling there."

"And did you see her, Your Honor?" Poor Hodge wasn't sure how to address the Count, and this phrase seemed to serve as well as another.

The Count shook his head. "No. I find later that she is in the parlor."

Asked what path he had taken, he said he had gone along the central path and looked into little clearings along the way, then turned left at the back of the garden.

"It is there, under the elm tree, that I see the body. I bend over and raise the head, and I see it is Richard, the husband of my wife's cousin. I shake his arm and try to rouse him, but to no avail. I bend to hear if there is breath, and there is none. That is when I hurry to the house to summon assistance."

"Did you see the dagger at that time, sir?"

"I did, yes, but only the gleam of the jewels. Until the torches came, I could not see well."

Now it was Carla's turn. When the Sheriff addressed her, she burst into tears and hid her face in her hands. So, I thought, where *was* our dear little Carla? At least she wasn't making love with Richard in the shrubbery.

Startled, as we all were, Hodge said, "What is it, madam?"

The Count said, apologetically, "My wife is easily frightened." Turning to Carla, he said gently, "You must answer the questions, my dear."

Handkerchief in hand, Carla sniffled but looked up at Hodge with a soulful expression. "I went for a stroll in the garden. It must have been some time before eleven, because I heard the bells as I sat in a little dell off the middle path."

"Did you see the deceased—that is, Master Richard Quiney or any other person at that time?"

Her voice trembling, she whispered, "I didn't see Richard, no."

"Do you mean that you saw someone else in the garden at that time?"

"Not then, but when I first went into the garden."

"And who was that person, madam?"

Carla covered her face with her hands. "No, no, I cannot say!"

"Madam, if you have information, you must tell what it is."

More sobs and wringing of hands. "No, no, I cannot!"

Now George Camden spoke firmly. "Contessa, if you know anything at all, you are obliged by law to reveal it."

Carla looked frightened. "You mean, *I must tell?*"

"Yes, you must."

"Well, then, I saw someone in the garden. He had the dagger in his sleeve. I saw the jewels flashing."

Hodge raised his pencil over his notebook. "And who was this person, madam?"

More protests and urgings, and finally Carla came out with it. "It was Master Shakespeare!"

"And where was Master Shakespeare when you saw him?"

Another sob. "He was walking along the garden path toward the corner with the elm tree."

"That is the place where the body was found?"

There was shocked silence in the room. Then all eyes turned toward Will, who simply shook his head, looking surprised but mildly amused. "I'm afraid the lady is mistaken. I never at any time had the dagger in my possession nor did I go in that direction."

Will may be amused, I thought, but I'm not. What was Carla up to, practically accusing Will of murder?

The Sheriff then asked Carla, "Did Master Shakespeare see you or speak to you?"

"Oh, no, he didn't know I was there."

"And what did you do after this time, madam?"

She seemed calmer now and replied that she had remained in the little dell for some time. Yes, she had heard footsteps going by but she did not see the person nor could she have been seen where she was. Then she had come back to the house.

That was all they could get from Carla, but it was pretty startling.

Then the Sheriff's men came back to report that no stranger had been seen nor heard of in the town. Still, George remarked that a local person could have entered through the open gate, and the Sheriff looked puzzled.

"Begging your pardon, Master Camden, but it don't seem as how a person could have come through t' gate in back and in t' house and took t' dagger from t' table without being seen?"

George nodded. "I'm afraid you are right, Sheriff, but it is possible that someone in the house—one of the servants, perhaps—took the dagger from the table and passed it to someone at the gate."

The Sheriff nodded solemnly, making a note on his paper.

At last, the Sheriff went off to question the servants, and the others gradually took their leave, the Count throwing his cloak protectively around his wife as he led her away.

When Will and I lay in bed talking that night, he scoffed at the whole thing, and I said the only comfort was that Carla probably wouldn't make a very reliable witness.

I couldn't have been more wrong.

The next afternoon, before the Magistrate, Carla stuck to her story. Will was asked who was the gentleman he had been speaking with, but he didn't know. The man was a stranger.

George Camden, who had come to represent Will, asked the Magistrate to delay until the stranger could be located, but Sheriff Hodge declared that his men had been inquiring and searching all morning and had found no trace of a stranger in the town. He didn't have to remind us that strangers are always noticed in a town the size of Stratford.

Now the Magistrate adopted a formal tone. "In a case of this kind, I do not determine the guilt or innocence of a person accused of a crime. It is my sole duty to make a determination whether or not a trial should be held to present the evidence and to arrive at a verdict. In the present case, such a course is indicated."

And so the inconceivable happened. William Shakespeare was charged with the murder of Richard Quiney. George Camden, as Will's defense counsel, asked for bail, but it was denied because the charge was murder.

I felt as if I was trapped in a nightmare as I saw two men take hold of Will's arms and lead him off to a prison cell.

Chapter 5

TRIAL

i

When I visited Will in the local jail in Stratford, we went through every phase of disbelief. How could this have happened? And, since Will didn't do it, who in fact had killed Richard? There were plenty of people who hated Richard, but there wasn't a shred of evidence against any one of them, so far as we knew. All the members of the company, especially those still wearing their costumes, had been questioned and declared they had left the party well before the tolling of eleven hours. But could one of them have slipped back through the garden gate? And why?

And what about Carla? Did she really believe she had seen Will with the dagger? Or was it simply one of those hallucinations she was so fond of? I was terrified when I thought that innocent people had been convicted before. This could actually happen to Will.

George Camden had one bit of good news. The Court of Assizes, which travels quarterly around Warwickshire to try serious crimes, was in session in the month of July, and the case could be heard without delay.

All right, I thought, if there's anything that can be done, we'll do it now.

I went back to the house, where Susanna and Judith, along with David and young Doctor Hall, were waiting to hear the news of Will.

"The trial may be in a few days," I told them.

Judith said eagerly, "Can we do anything to help, Mama?"

"Yes," I said, "I think you can. We need to find the old gentleman Papa was talking with in the garden. The police say they haven't found him, but that doesn't mean he isn't still around somewhere."

Susanna nodded and turned to the young doctor. "We can do that! John, can you help?"

"Absolutely! I have done my morning calls and I'm free for awhile."

David said, "Good! Then let's work out how to start."

Susanna said, "We must get Agnes too."

But David shook his head. "She is sitting with Mama, who seems to be in a bad way. I'm sure she won't leave her."

And the four of them set off eagerly to make their plans.

My hope was that if they found the man and he confirmed Will's statement, the charges against Will might be dropped. But would that be enough? What if the man was found but he wasn't aware of the time? Or might he have left sooner than Will recalled? Or he might be forgetful, like so many elderly persons, and not remember clearly what had taken place.

Well, I told myself firmly, never mind "what if." Let's do something positive.

My own first plan of action was to have a talk with Carla. She and the Count were staying at Rosanna's place, as usual on their visits. I would speak to Rosanna first and then tackle Carla.

When I got to the house, I found Agnes anxiously hovering about the door.

"I saw you coming," she said, her voice trembling. "I'm so glad you're here. I don't know what to do with Mama."

I knew Rosanna would be shocked by the events of the last evening, but I didn't expect that she would be in deep grief over Richard. Yet, how do we know how people really feel when a death occurs?

"What does she say, Agnes?"

Her dark eyes looked frightened. "She won't say anything. Just sits there looking stunned. Did she really care about him after all?"

"We don't know, do we?"

Still troubled, Agnes said, "She's in the garden. See what you think, Anne."

I found Rosanna reclining in a cushioned chair, looking out toward the back of our old house in Henley Street. When I sat down beside her, she didn't move or answer my greeting. I put my hand gently on her arm.

"Rosanna."

Slowly, her head turned and she looked at me in surprise. "Anne?"

"Yes, dear. I am so sorry about Richard."

Her head turned slightly, so that she was gazing again at our old house. "We used to have a gate there, didn't we?"

I smiled. "Yes, we did."

Silence. Then, "The children played together, didn't they?"

"Yes, dear."

Another pause. "Every day?"

"Yes, every day."

"And we were together, you and I?"

I pressed her hand. "Of course we were."

Then she looked up at me. "I wouldn't hurt Richard, would I?"

Baffled, I said, "No, I'm sure you wouldn't."

She sighed and closed her eyes, and I quietly slipped away.

Agnes was waiting, trembling with anxiety. "What do you think I should do?"

I felt as helpless as Agnes did. "I wish I knew," I said. "I believe we must simply wait. Perhaps it's best if we don't try to make her speak until she is ready. She will come round eventually, I'm sure."

"Yes, you're right. We will have to be patient. But surely it isn't because of Richard, is it? I mean, I would have thought she would be *glad* that someone—I mean glad that he is dead."

I thought of how forgiving Rosanna had always been, and wondered if his death had somehow revived her early love for the wretched man, but I didn't suggest this to Agnes. I merely said again that we would wait.

I told her that the other young people were out searching for the old gentleman that Will met in the garden the night of the murder. Asked if she wanted to join them, she said, "No, I must stay with Mama."

I put my arms around her. "Don't worry, my dear. I'll go up now and speak to Carla."

I made my way upstairs. The servant had told me, to my great relief, that the Count was not at home, and I found Carla curled up in a deep chair, sipping chocolate and nibbling biscuits.

"Hello, Anne," she said.

I took a chair facing her. "All right, Carla. What kind of game are you playing?"

Big, dark eyes opened in surprise. "Whatever do you mean?"

"I mean saying that you saw Will in the garden with the dagger in his sleeve."

"But I did, Anne. I *saw* him."

"Now, Carla, do you remember telling us that you saw a vision of your dead grandmother at your house in Siena?"

"Of course. I did see her."

"And that she faded into the stone wall and disappeared?"

She shivered. "Yes, that's true, Anne."

"And you know that what you saw was what is called a ghost, and that it was not real? Hasn't Antonio told you that? You surely believe him, don't you?"

Eyelids lowered, she whispered, "Yes, but he says I am not telling a lie."

"Yes. He means that you truly *believe* what you saw, isn't that so?"

A meek nod.

"Right. Then don't you understand that that is what happened when you saw Will in the garden?"

Now her eyes flashed in anger. "No, it was not the same at all. I know what I saw, and you can't make me say I didn't!"

I kept my patient tone. "Now, Carla, I want you to think about something. Do you know that Will has been arrested and is in prison, accused of killing Richard Quiney?"

"Yes."

"There will be a trial in a few days, and you will have to stand up in front of the judge and the lawyers and all the people in the courtroom and tell this story. And if they believe you, then Will may be sent to prison for many years. Do you want that to happen?"

She reached out for a biscuit and put it in her mouth.

"Carla! Pay attention! Now, look at me. Do you want Will to go to prison?"

Sullen. "No."

"Then you must tell the truth."

Another protest that she is not lying.

I tried another tack. "Carla, have you any reason to dislike Will?"

Now her eyes flashed again. "Of course not, why do you think that?"

"If you do not, then try to think about this. If you realize that what you saw just might be partly in your imagination, even though it is very real to you, would you just say that in the courtroom? It could help very much when it goes to the jury if they see that there is even a little doubt. Can you do that, Carla?"

Now she looked at me as if she had gained a triumph over me. "You think I'm so stupid, Anne, but you are trying to make me tell lies, and I won't do it. I can see through you better than you think I can."

Now I let my own anger show. "I never said you were stupid, Carla. I think you are a crafty little liar—"

At that moment, I heard footsteps on the stair and the Count came into the room.

Carla cried out, "Antonio!" and threw herself into his arms. I expected a blast of anger from him, but instead he looked at me with a curious expression I did not understand. He held Carla tenderly in his arms, kissed the top of her head, then gently patted her arm.

"Wait here, dearest," he said. "I shall just speak to Anne for a moment and I shall be back."

Carla gave me a look that said, "You see, you can't bully me with Antonio here."

The Count followed me down the stairs to a wide landing, where I stopped and stood by the window. Outside, a pale sun wavered among watery clouds, and I watched as the townspeople went about their daily tasks, and the swans on the river darted among the boats, snatching for food.

I turned to the Count with a look of appeal. "Can you help me, Antonio?"

"I want to help you," he said, "but I am troubled to know what to do."

"That's simple enough," I said sharply. "Tell Carla to drop this nonsense of seeing Will with the dagger. You don't believe her yourself, do you?"

He frowned. "How can I be sure? She truly believes that is what she saw. It may be that in the court, they will also not be sure, and then they will not say that Will is guilty, do you see?"

"Well, I see that would be fine if it happens, but what if they *do* believe her, and that is the thing that makes them convict him?"

He looked at me, his face troubled. "But you see, Mistress Anne, I am certain that the jury will know that Will is a famous and honorable man, and they will believe he is innocent. In Italia, that would have great weight in people's minds."

Well, I thought, that's all very well in Italy, but this is England, and people are not likely to let an accused person go free just because he is famous. In fact, one of my worries was that the jury of Will's "peers" might very well feel resentment, even jealousy, over his rise to fame and fortune.

I said nothing of this to the Count, however, and it looked to me as if he was too obsessed with his dear Carla to be of much help to me.

He patted my arm. "I am sure Will will not be found guilty, Anne."

I simply shook my head and went on down the stairs, where I found Agnes in the small parlor. She had obviously been weeping. She still clutched a sodden handkerchief, and her eyes looked haggard.

I tried soothing murmurs, but at last she came out with it, repeating what she had hinted at earlier. "Oh, Anne, I truly thought Mama would be glad that Richard was gone. He was so bad. He struck her—"

"And you, too," I added.

"Yes, and then he made love to her cousin. I hated him so much. *I'm glad he's dead.* I thought Mama would be glad, too, but now she won't say a word."

"Maybe she is glad, Agnes. We don't know what she is feeling just now, do we? And don't forget that the dear cousin she loves was just as guilty as Richard."

"Yes, you're right. I hate her too, and I never thought, when I was a child, that I would ever hate anybody! It's different when you are grown up, isn't it?"

I agreed, acknowledging that at nineteen, Agnes and Susanna were indeed adults, and mature ones at that.

I went out to the garden and tried speaking to Rosanna again but got no response, and taking my own advice to Agnes, I gave up and started toward home.

Beyond the Guild Hall, I encountered Judith and David, who reported that they were searching the byways and back alleys in the town.

Judith said, "We are asking people if they have seen an old man in a long gray cloak, and we are looking into places where he might have been staying."

And David added, "No one so far has mentioned that the police had already asked them about this, so I don't think they have tried very hard to find him, as they claim."

"I can believe that," I said. "Once they have a culprit, and they believe he is guilty, they are not likely to look for another one."

"Of course the man may have left town, so Susanna and the doctor are riding out along the roads to ask at the farms if he has been seen."

I left them studying their map of Stratford, marking areas not yet searched.

Slowly, I walked on, longing for some consolation. I was not far from George Camden's office, when I remembered a question I had wanted to ask him. I found him deep in his law books.

"Hello, Anne. I'm hoping to find a precedent for a case hinging on an unreliable witness."

"That's our Carla, all right," I said bitterly. "I've just been working on her and she's holding firm. Antonio admitted to me that he isn't sure whether he believes her or not."

"Good. I can work that angle at the trial if I have to. One problem, of course, is that Carla is a pretty woman, and the jurors are all male."

I grimaced. "How true that is."

Then I added, "George, I've been wondering about whether we might raise the question of the size and strength that would be required for anyone to stab Richard in the back in that fashion. Could we suggest it must have been a tall person?"

George frowned. "I've been thinking about that, Anne, and I'm afraid that won't do. Look, take this pen." He handed me a long quill from his desk. "Now, raise your arm as high as you can. Remember that the dagger is pointed and very sharp, and it is at least a foot in length. I believe even you could do it."

He stood in front of me, raising his toes to give him extra height.

"Now. Try!"

I too stretched to my full height, and allowing extra inches for George, I saw that it was just possible that I could stab him.

"You're right," I said. "It could be done."

He added, "And Will is of average height, not a small man at all, and his arms are strong."

I nodded. "Yes, I see. That won't work."

George tried to look reassuring, but his voice shook. "I'll do everything in my power to prove Will didn't do this, Anne. He *must be acquitted!*" I was surprised at his vehemence but glad he cared so much.

As I walked on through the town, I saw Edward Bushell in the high street and signaled to him to wait for me. I saw him turn his head, as if to pretend he hadn't seen me, but I spoke his name, and he had to stand until I came up to him.

"I've just been to see your sister, Edward. Are you going there now?"

"Oh, yes, presently. Yes, of course. Dreadful thing about Richard. Oh, dear."

"And a dreadful thing about Will, too. You know he is charged with the murder?"

Edward shrank back as if I had struck him. "Oh, yes, quite shocking. Surely he didn't—that is, I'm sure he couldn't have—"

"Killed Richard? No, Edward, he did not. I need to know who *did* do it. Who do you think it could have been?"

"Who do *I* think? Oh, I have no idea, Anne. How could I possibly know? I must go to Rosanna now. Goodbye." And he scurried off.

I was not far from Libby Russell's house, and I thought about young Tom Quiney's story of seeing Libby and Richard making love. Could the boy have misunderstood? Exaggerated what he actually saw?

I knocked at the door and the motherly servant greeted me with a cheerful smile. "She seems a bit better today."

I found Libby sitting in her usual chair, staring vacantly at the wall. When she saw me, she did nod her head and put out a hand as if in welcome, and I had to admit that was an improvement over the last time I had seen her.

No use making small talk. I said without preamble, "Libby, do you know that Richard Quiney is dead?"

"Oh, yes, of course he is."

Now she seemed more animated. "You see, everyone I care for is dead. My Mama died, my baby died, my dear Jeb died. Now Richard died."

Surprised, I asked, "Did you care for Richard, Libby?"

"Of course I did. He was so kind."

A radiant smile lighted her pretty face. "He told me he had always loved me, even before I married Jeb. And sometimes he came into bed with me, and it was wonderful. I felt alive again, and warm. I am always so cold, you see."

Then she looked thoughtful. "Poor Richard. People were so unkind to him. He always needed money, and I always gave him whatever he asked for, and he was so grateful."

I bet he was, I thought.

Then her voice dropped again. "But of course, I knew he would die, like all the others."

"Did you know that Tom saw you with his father?"

"Tom? I don't know. He left some flowers for me one day. He is a dear boy. Was Richard here that day?"

In a few minutes, I bent and kissed the top of her head and quietly slipped away.

At least one person mourned for Richard, I thought bitterly.

So Tom was not wrong about what he had seen that day. But there was another question I needed to ask.

I walked down to the river and along the path to Holy Trinity Church, where I found Tom and the sexton digging a new grave. Horrified, I stepped back and stared. Surely it couldn't be—?

Tom set down his shovel when he saw me. "It's all right, Anne. Yes, it is for Papa, and I *wanted* to do this."

This was no time to ask him the question that troubled me. It could wait. I gave him a hug and went home.

Then we got the news from George Camden that the trial would be held the next day. Apparently the previous trial of the Court of Assizes had ended sooner than expected and they had come directly to Stratford, to be ready to start Will's trial in the morning.

Our young people hadn't found so much as a trace of the old gentleman who had talked with Will in the garden the night of the murder.

Susanna frowned. "He must have left the town, or surely someone would have seen or heard something of him."

George greeted us with the news that the judge would be Lord Wendell. "He's notoriously bad-tempered and irascible," he told us, "and as if that's not enough, we have Sir Henry Utley for the Crown, who is a sly little weasel. He's been here since noon, talking with the Magistrate and the Sheriff, and preparing his case. We shall have our work cut out to deal with him."

ii

I spent a miserable night, wavering between fear of the worst and hope that something might emerge at the trial to help Will's cause. The next morning was a day of brilliant sunshine. Dark clouds would have seemed more fitting to me.

The judge and all his retinue had been housed at the Swan Inn, and now they marched along in a glittering procession, surrounded by noisy crowds gawking at their finery. They passed directly in front of our house in Chapel Street just as we stepped out the door, and we waited till they were gone before walking quietly on to Church Street and into the Guild Hall.

In the Hall, the throne-like chair for the presiding judge had been placed on the raised dais, with the witness box to the judge's right, the dock for the accused opposite, the jury at the judge's left, and the tables for the Queen's prosecutor and for the defendant's lawyer facing the judge. A railing separated the court from the rows of spectators, and needless to say, everybody in town was there, gaping at the spectacle of their famous citizen on trial for a heinous crime. Seeing a play about murder was exciting enough, but what could be better than the real thing?

The proceedings began with the seating of the twelve members of the jury. Since Will held the status of Gentleman, his peers were all of that rank and had been gathered from Stratford and the surrounding area. Then Will was brought in and placed in the dock, and the Clerk of the Court read the charge, that "the prisoner, William Shakespeare, did cause the death of Richard Quiney, resident of Stratford-upon-Avon, by stabbing the victim with a dagger."

The judge, sour-faced and frowning, bent toward Will. "How do you plead?"

"I am not guilty, your Lordship."

The judge all but snorted, then turned to the prosecutor for the Crown. "Sir Henry, you may proceed."

"Thank you, your Lordship."

"Weasel" was a good description, I thought. Sir Henry was a small man, with thinning hair and a high-pitched voice. Addressing the jury, he stated simply that on the 10th day of July in the present year, Master William Shakespeare had committed the crime of which he was accused. The Crown would present witnesses who would testify to his presence at or near the victim at the time of the murder, with the murder weapon in his possession, and other witnesses who would indicate the motives that led the prisoner to commit this foul deed.

The first witness was Sheriff Hodge, who described arriving at the scene, examining the deceased, and directing his men to carry the body to the Quiney residence. He had then questioned all of those present, including the servants. He described how the jeweled dagger had been shown to the various guests and had been laid on a table, although at what time was not known, nor did anyone admit to seeing the dagger again. He reported that all the members of the actors' company had departed soon after the hour of ten. Then no one recalled seeing Richard Quiney after the bells tolled eleven hours, and it was approximately a quarter of an hour after that when the body was found.

Sir Henry cleared his throat. "Now, Sheriff, will you please tell us what caused you to detain Master Shakespeare on this charge?"

Hodge looked solemn. "Yes, sir. A lady stated as she had seen Master Shakespeare walking in the garden and she could see the jeweled dagger in his sleeve."

"At what time was this?"

"The lady was not sure, but she thought as it was shortly before eleven hours."

"And what did the prisoner say, when confronted with this information?"

"He said as he had been in conversation with an old gentleman, a stranger, at t' back gate of t' garden."

"And can you produce the gentleman in question?"

Hodge frowned. "No, sir. We have asked everywhere, and there is no sign of such a person."

The judge leaned forward and intoned, *"No sign of such a person?"*

Hodge swallowed. "That is correct, your Lordship. Most times a stranger in the town is noticed, as you might say, but we can find no trace of him."

"And how hard did you try?" I muttered to myself.

The next witness was Carla's husband, the Count. As he stood in the witness box and took the oath to tell the truth, he made an impressive appearance, with his thick, silvered hair and distinguished demeanor. He gave his name in a rich baritone. "I am Antonio Baldini, Conte di Lucca."

"Now, sir, will you please describe what occurred at the home of the prisoner, Master Shakespeare, on the night in question?"

"Yes. I go into the large garden behind the house and walk along the paths. I am looking for my wife, thinking she may have strolled into the garden."

"At what time was this?"

"It was after the bells had tolled for eleven hours. I do not know how much after. When I come to the corner of the garden, under a large tree, I see a man lying face down on the ground. I bend over him and shake his arm, but he does not move. Then I lift his head and I see that he is Richard, the husband of my wife's cousin. Now I believe he is dead."

"What made you believe so?"

Antonio shrugged. "He does not breathe. And on the back of his coat is much blood."

"Did you see anything else?"

"Yes. The dagger with the jewels is lying on the ground beside him. So I go quickly to the house to tell what I have found."

"Did you see anyone else in the garden?"

"No, but as I come to the house, I see Master Shakespeare coming toward the terrazzo."

"The terrace?"

"Si, the terrace. But he is on the far side of the garden, nowhere near where the dead man is lying."

Sir Henry turned to George Camden. "Your witness."

George rose and looked at Antonio with a friendly expression.

"Good day, Count. Can you tell us, did Master Shakespeare appear to be walking rapidly toward the house?"

"No, sir, not at all. He is what you call strolling, and when he sees me, he raises a hand in greeting. But I shout to him what has happened, and then he runs. He calls to his wife to send the menservants to us and he follows me to where Richard is lying."

The Count was dismissed, and his wife was called to the box. Carla was wearing a simple dress of dark brown, with no jewelry, her hair in a single coil on her head. Her face was pale, and she stood, clutching the rail of the witness box, her voice trembling as she gave her name. What an act, I thought. Too bad women are not allowed to perform on the stage. Carla would be a winner.

Sir Henry gave a respectful little bow. "Now, Countess, if you will please tell us what you saw in the garden on the evening in question."

In a piteous whisper, Carla said, "I saw Master Shakespeare walking in the garden."

The judge's voice cut in. "Speak up, madam."

Sir Henry repeated, "You saw Master Shakespeare walking in the garden?"

"Yes."

"At what time was this?"

"I believe it was before when the bells ring for the hour of eleven."

"And did you speak to him?"

"No. I could see him through the foliage but he did not see me."

"I see. And what did you see that has a bearing upon the present inquiry?"

Big eyes, looking soulful. "I saw the handle of a dagger in his sleeve. It had many jewels on it."

All eyes in the courtroom turned to the table on which a jeweled dagger, its blade in a sheath, sat on a satin cloth. Sir Henry picked it up and held it aloft. "Like this one?"

"Yes."

"Had you seen a dagger like this before?"

"Yes. We had all been looking at it earlier in the evening when it was taken out of the glass case in the parlor. But I am sure it means nothing—"

Sir Henry cut her off. "That is for the jury to decide." And he returned to his seat.

George Camden rose slowly and spoke in a sympathetic tone. "We understand this must be most distressing for you, Countess. Now, I believe that there had been a performance of the play, *Julius Caesar*, before the gathering at the Shakespeare home. Do you recall the part that was played by Master Shakespeare?"

"Yes. He played the part of Julius Caesar."

"Exactly. And I believe at one point in the play that character is stabbed to death by a group of his associates. Is that correct?"

Carla whispered, "Yes."

"And later in the play, the character of Caesar appears again, wearing a white shroud, to indicate the form of a ghost, is that correct?"

Carla gave a little shudder. "Yes."

"And I believe Master Shakespeare was still in his costume during the reception which followed."

"Yes, but not in the white shroud."

George paused, looking around the courtroom with a slight smile.

"No, not in the shroud, to be sure. That would have been an awkward mode of dress for such an occasion, would it not?"

There was a sprinkle of titters among the spectators, and the judge frowned fiercely.

George turned back to Carla. "Now, madam, we are agreed that Master Shakespeare was wearing the costume of Caesar as it was at the beginning of the play?"

"Yes."

"Is it not possible that the dagger you saw might have been a part of that costume?"

I drew in a breath at this, because the daggers used in the play were not jeweled, but George no doubt hoped to confuse Carla with the question.

She did look startled, but she shook her head and said she was sure it was the dagger from the glass case she had seen. "The jewels were very bright, even in the dim light in the garden."

"Now, is it not possible that you have in your mind the image of Master Shakespeare in the play and that that made you believe you saw him in reality?"

Carla looked confused, then said, "No, I saw him. I am not mistaken."

Now George turned as if to sit down, then turned back as an afterthought. "Countess, can you tell us whether the dagger was in the sleeve of the left or the right arm of Master Shakespeare?"

Carla blinked, then pointed to her own right arm. "This one," she said without hesitation.

"You indicate the right arm. Now, let us try a little experiment. If a man picks up a dagger like this one . . ." And with a quick movement, George picked up the dagger and held it in his right hand. "If, as I say, a man who uses his right hand by habit wishes to place this in the sleeve of his coat, it would be natural to do this." He deftly slid the dagger into the sleeve of his left arm.

"But if the man uses his left hand by habit, he would do this." He held the dagger in his left hand and inserted it into his right sleeve. "Now, Master Shakespeare happens to use his right hand by habit. It is unlikely that he would place an object into his right sleeve."

Carla looked frightened. "I am not sure . . . I may have been mistaken. Perhaps it was the other sleeve."

George said quietly, "Yes, you may have been mistaken. No further questions." He sat down, and Carla was excused.

I asked George later how he knew Carla would point to the right arm, and he said most people point to the right when asked, but if she hadn't, he would simply have dropped the question.

The next two witnesses were John Heminges and Henry Condell, the two actors in Will's company who were his especially congenial friends. John Heminges was called to the stand first. We knew how reluctant they both were to testify, and Sir Henry knew it too. He began with establishing that the witness was a member of the Lord Chamberlain's theater company, along with the defendant. Then he asked with a sly smile, "You were acquainted with the deceased?"

Heminges looked at him with innocent eyes. "Yes, sir, but he was not deceased at the time."

A smothered titter swept through the spectators, and the judge bent over to Heminges. "There will be no levity in this courtroom, sir."

Heminges bowed respectfully.

Sir Henry, repressing his anger, said, "Please state the circumstances of your acquaintance with Richard Quiney."

"Yes, sir. The gentleman often attended the theater in London in the company of his friend, Master Bushell, and he sometimes came onto the stage after the performance."

"Thank you. Now, will you please describe an incident that occurred on one such occasion between Richard Quiney and the prisoner at the bar?"

"There was a slight altercation between the two. Nothing of any importance."

Sir Henry looked at the jury with raised eyebrows. "Is it not true that Master Shakespeare struck the deceased—er, that is, Richard Quiney—with his fist?"

"Yes, I believe he did."

"And is it not true that the two men grappled together and that you and other members of your company found it necessary to pull them apart?"

"Yes. We did not want any damage to the stage."

Another titter, and a scowl from his Lordship.

"Are you aware of the cause of the quarrel between the two men?"

"No, sir."

"Did you hear Master Shakespeare make a threat to his adversary?"

"Just the sort of thing a man may say in the anger of the moment."

Sir Henry's voice rose to a squeal. "We do not wish to hear your interpretation. We wish to hear the words that were uttered."

"Oh, of course. Will said something about bashing Richard's head in if the problem recurred."

" *'Bashing his head in.'* Thank you, Mr. Heminges. That will be all."

Camden waved his hand. "No questions."

Then Henry Condell took the stand and corroborated the previous testimony, giving a skilled performance of a man who is highly amused by all the nonsense but who duly answers whatever he is asked.

The next witness called was Edward Bushell. Poor Edward dithered and stumbled at each question, looking at Sir Henry with timid eyes.

Sir Henry began, "What was your relation to the deceased, please?"

Edward's voice shook. "My relation? Oh, I see, yes, he was the husband of my sister, Mistress Rosanna Wilson."

"Was she not Rosanna Quiney?"

"Oh, dear. Yes, of course, she became that when they married."

"Exactly. Now, were you on good terms with the deceased?"

"Good terms? Oh, yes, certainly."

Sir Henry gave him a cold look. "Master Bushell, I can produce witnesses to the contrary. Please remember that you are under oath."

Edward literally choked, coughing into a large handkerchief. "Yes, well, we had been good friends for many years. Then we had a falling out, so to speak."

"And what was the cause of this 'falling out'?"

"It was a personal matter."

"I see. And you were very angry with the deceased, were you not?"

"Yes," Edward croaked. "Yes, I was very angry."

"Is it not true, Master Bushell, that you were a member of the party that attempted to overthrow Her Majesty the Queen by armed rebellion?"

Trembling, Edward whispered, "Yes, I did contribute money, but I did not take part in the actual attack."

With a look of utmost contempt, Sir Henry said, "No, I am sure you did not."

Now Sir Henry raised his voice. "Is it not true that you believed that the deceased, Richard Quiney, had taken action to betray the cause you espoused? And that that is the cause of your anger against him?"

"Yes."

Now Sir Henry paused, looked up at the ceiling, then glanced at the jury. "And did you confide this matter to anyone else?"

Edward looked over at Will, where he stood in the dock, and whispered, "Yes, I told my friend Will Shakespeare."

I gave a start, and Rosanna pressed my hand, giving me a look of apology for her brother. Friend indeed, I thought. Damn Edward.

"And what was the response of your friend on learning of the matter?"

"He was also very angry with Richard."

"Did he express any threat to Master Quiney?"

"Oh, not really a threat. He didn't mean anything—"

The judge leaned forward and spoke sternly. "Please

state the words spoken by the accused."

Edward choked, then sighed. "He said he would like to have Richard at the point of his sword."

"Thank you. No further questions." Sir Henry gave a triumphant glance at the jury and took his seat.

George rose. "Now, Master Bushell, how long ago did this conversation take place?"

Edward blinked. "When? It was before I went abroad. That was in the month of March."

"In the month of March. And it is now the month of July. And have you been in the presence of Master Shakespeare and Richard Quiney since that time?"

"Yes, certainly."

"And what was Master Shakespeare's demeanor toward Quiney on those occasions?"

"Well, much the same as usual."

"He showed no particular animosity toward Quiney?"

"He didn't like Richard, but he wasn't rude to him."

"And what of your own feelings, Master Bushell? Have you also felt some animosity toward Quiney?"

Now Edward's voice was strong and clear. "I never forgave him for what he did. I was civil to him only for the sake of my sister."

"Is it possible that you, too, would have liked to have Richard Quiney 'at the point of your sword'?"

Edward shrank back, eyes full of terror. "Oh, I would never—that is, I wouldn't have dared—"

George let the words hang in the air. Then with a look of utter contempt, he said, "Thank you, Mr. Bushell. That will be all."

Sir Henry shrugged and waved a hand. Then he rose with an air of importance and turned to the jury. "Gentlemen, it is time to summarize for you the case against the prisoner. This should take very little time. It is clear to you by now that he was seen in the garden, with the dagger in his sleeve, on or about the hour of eleven. It is also clear that no one in the party that evening recalls seeing Richard Quiney after that hour, except of course the prisoner himself."

Sir Henry allowed himself a little smile. "Need I point out to you that we have only his word for this. His story of having a prolonged conversation with an elderly gentleman who has been seen by absolutely no one except the prisoner is scarcely credible. You have also been shown that the prisoner felt strong animosity toward the victim. While it is not necessary for the Crown to provide a motive for this crime, such knowledge will inevitably assist you in reaching a verdict in this case."

Sir Henry took his seat with a self-satisfied smirk, and George Camden rose for the defense.

"Gentlemen of the jury," he began, "you have heard evidence that would appear to cast suspicion upon Master William Shakespeare as the perpetrator of this crime, but what, after all, does it amount to? Place yourselves at the occasion on the evening in question. A large number of persons is present in a house with many reception rooms, where people may move about freely, and at the back is a spacious garden, with paths that wind through thick shrubbery and trees. It is very dark in the garden by the hour of eleven. Anyone in the party may wander into and out of the garden unobserved unless by a chance encounter.

"The Countess Baldini is the cousin of Richard Quiney's wife, Rosanna, and of Master Edward Bushell, her brother. The Countess has told you that she saw Master Shakespeare in the garden, with the dagger in his sleeve. She is confused about which sleeve. She may also be confused about what she actually saw in the darkness. While she is a very pleasant lady, the Countess is given to fancies, reporting to her friends and acquaintances that she has seen the ghosts of various persons from time to time. She believes these to be true events. During the performance of the play that very day, Master Shakespeare played the role of Julius Caesar. At one time he appeared, draped in a shroud, to simulate a ghost. The Countess was seen to be excessively frightened at this apparition, apparently fearing that it was real. We must bear this in mind before concluding that her report of what she saw that evening can be relied upon.

"As for the quarrel between Master Shakespeare and Richard Quiney on the stage of the theater in London, is it likely that such an episode would lead to the act of murder after many months had passed with no further sign of animosity on the part of the accused?

"The same may be said for Edward Bushell's report of Master Shakespeare's anger over a matter which seemed to have no lasting result."

At this point, Camden paused and looked gravely at the jurors. "It is obvious, however, that Master Bushell himself did retain extreme animosity toward his sister's husband. Is it not possible—?"

Sir Henry leaped to his feet, squeaking, "Your Lordship?"

And the judge treated George to a glare that was meant to intimidate. "Master Camden," he growled, "may I remind you that your client is the person on trial here. We will have no more of this!"

George tried to look chastened. "Of course, your Lordship. I believe the time has come for us to hear the truth of the matter from the defendant himself."

There was a stir in the courtroom, as all eyes turned to Will, standing in the dock.

George said, "Master Shakespeare, will you please tell the Court in your own words what occurred on the evening of the murder?"

My heart gave a leap as Will's wonderful voice filled the room. "Yes. When all the members of my company had departed, and I had talked with a few of the remaining guests, I strolled out into the garden to enjoy the cool air. I walked along the path that leads to a bench near the back gate and sat down to rest. Then I noticed that the gate was ajar, and when I peered out, I was surprised to see a gentleman standing there. I said, 'Good evening,' and he replied in such a pleasant voice that I engaged him in conversation. He was a tall man, wearing a long cloak, with a hood that had fallen back, revealing a shock of white hair. He told me that he was a stranger, just passing through the town, that he had lived in the area long ago and had wanted to visit it again. I invited him to come into the garden, and we sat on the bench under the linden tree.

"Presently, we heard footsteps coming rather rapidly along the path, and I saw that it was Richard Quiney. I said, 'Richard?' and he looked startled. He muttered something I didn't hear and hurried on, taking the path leading across to the far corner of the garden by the elm tree. My companion surprised me by asking, 'Is that Richard Quiney?' and when I said it was, he remarked that he remembered him from when he was a lad.

"It was just at that point that the bells began to ring for the hour of eleven. We went on talking for quite some time. The old gentleman asked about myself, and I was so taken with his gentle manner that I told him my name and a bit about my family and my life in London, but when I asked him about himself, he said there were reasons why he could not disclose his identity. He said, 'That is why I come out only at night,' and there was such sorrow in his voice that I felt pity for whatever tragedy had blighted his life. He told me that he had lived abroad for many years, and that he would be returning there very soon. Then his face lighted with a smile, and he said, 'I have found what I came for, and now I may go.' "

There was a hush in the courtroom when Will stopped speaking, and George Camden sat silent, allowing Will's words to linger in the air.

Then he rose and asked quietly, "One question, Master Shakespeare. During the time you sat with the elderly stranger, did you hear voices or sounds from other parts of the garden?"

"Yes, there were the usual sounds of footsteps and dim voices as people moved about. I believe once or twice one could hear laughter, but the shrubbery is thick and sounds are muffled. Of course, I have realized since that evening that Richard's death must have taken place during the time I sat with the old gentleman, but I heard nothing like a cry or a call for help. It was when the gentleman had thanked me for talking with him and gone out of the gate that I walked back toward the house, and as I came toward the terrace, I heard the Count shouting for help. That is all I know of what happened."

George took his seat, and we saw Sir Henry spring quickly to his feet to cross-examine. "This is all very well, Master Shakespeare, but it is obvious that we have only your word for all of this. We are aware that you are a clever writer of dramas. It would not be in the least surprising that you could invent this touching story of an old gentleman who appeared so conveniently, and has now apparently disappeared into thin air."

Now he turned to the jury. "Gentlemen, we must remember that the Sheriff and his men have combed the area, seeking any trace of this mythical person, with no success. We must also remember that the prisoner not only invents marvelous stories, he is also an experienced actor who can sway an audience with his performance on the stage."

Now it was George's turn to leap to his feet. "Your Honor, this is not cross-examination. This is argument to the jury."

The judge gave Sir Henry a tolerant little smile. "You are quite right, Master Camden. Sir Henry, you will please refrain from commentary."

Sir Henry bowed with mock humiliation.

Turning back to Will, he now raised his voice to its sharpest pitch. "I put it to you, Master writer and actor, that there is not a scintilla of truth is this story, that in fact you have felt anger at Richard Quiney for a very long time, anger that built to a point where you seized the opportunity, in the darkness of the garden, to wreak your vengeance upon him."

Now I felt a return of the terror that had gripped me off and on since the whole nightmare began. I knew Will was telling the truth, and those who knew him well would know the same, but what about those men on the jury? How much might there be among them of jealousy or resentment at Will's success? One of their peers had become rich and famous, and not everyone finds that pleasing. Often enough, people want to pull down those who have risen above them. And, worst of all, I had to admit that in a town like Stratford, a stranger couldn't be around for long without somebody seeing him.

Then I heard a sound behind where we sat, and turning, I saw a tall man in a gray cloak walking toward the court. He was wearing a large black cap that covered his head, and as he reached the railing, he pulled it off, revealing a head of white hair.

He looked up at the judge, and his voice was low but firm. "Your Lordship," he said, "I believe I am the man you are seeking."

The judge looked as startled as everyone else in the room. He then indicated to the clerk to put the stranger into the witness box.

First he turned to Will. "Is this the person of whom you spoke?"

Will looked at the man and said, "Yes, your Lordship, this is the gentleman."

The judge then turned to the old gentleman. "Please take the oath and state your name."

When he had given the oath, the man said, "My name is Roger Travers."

Now the judge asked him to tell the court what he had seen on the night in question.

His voice was gentle but carried clearly in the silent room. "I was walking along the lane behind a large house when I noticed a gate in the wall which was slightly ajar. I could hear the distant sound of music and voices, and I peered around the gate and stood listening for a moment. Then I saw the gentleman who is standing there in the dock. He spoke to me and we fell into conversation, as he has already described to you."

As he spoke to the court, I was only a few rows behind the railing, and directly in front of the witness box, and I stared into the face of the man. Why did he seem so familiar? And why was his voice so like a voice that I had known?

I caught my breath and suddenly I knew his name was not Roger Travers. For whatever reason, he could not give his true name, but I knew.

I made not a sound, but my lips formed the words. *Stephen! Stephen Brent!*

I stared at the white-haired stranger in the witness box. But Stephen was dead. How could it be Stephen?

In the voice that I remembered so well, he went on with his story, confirming in detail that he and Will did indeed have a conversation in the garden the night of the murder.

Sir Henry's tone dripped with skepticism. "And you would have us believe, sir, that you slipped away after this conversation with the accused and hid yourself in a place you cannot disclose until you learned that your companion was charged with murder?"

"Yes, that is correct."

"Now, sir, please describe the circumstance in which you saw—or claim you saw—the deceased, Richard Quiney."

"Certainly. A tall, strongly-built man came walking rapidly along the path near where we sat. Master Shakespeare said something like 'Richard?' and the man muttered a greeting and went on. I asked if that was Richard Quiney. I remembered him when he was a lad at school."

"That was a good many years ago, was it not? How could you recognize him in a dark garden after that length of time?"

"He was taller than the average man, and I recalled his vivid auburn hair."

Sir Henry rolled an eye at the jury, then went on. "At what time did this take place?"

"It was perhaps shortly after the man Quiney had passed us that the bells began to chime eleven hours. We then remained talking for a considerable time after that. I had just said goodnight and stepped out of the garden gate when I heard a shout for help from the other side of the garden."

"Now, sir, you say your name is Roger Travers. Will you please tell us your present place of residence?"

"I have been living abroad for many years."

"And in the days you have spent here in Stratford, where have you resided?"

"I have slept in the fields."

"I see. I believe this court will find it difficult to rely upon the testimony of an itinerant person with no known address. Is it not probable that, upon hearing the circumstances of this case talked about in the town, you have joined with the accused in concocting this story, perhaps for financial gain?"

"No. It all happened as I have described, but I see now that I must tell the full truth. I am a fugitive from the ecclesiastical courts. Long ago I was in prison on a charge of heresy. There was a breakout and I escaped to France, where I have lived until now."

The judge bent down and looked into the man's face. "Do you fully understand, sir, that if what you say is true, you will be arrested and given into the custody of the ecclesiastical authorities?"

"Yes, your Honor, I am aware of that."

"Then, why have you taken the risk of coming to the court now, sir?"

"I could not let an innocent man be convicted of a crime he did not commit."

There was stunned silence in the courtroom. Then George Camden rose. "Your Lordship, I move for a dismissal of the charges."

Now there was excitement and hubbub, everyone exclaiming about the astonishing turn of events.

The judge and the lawyers retired to an adjacent room,

while we waited in agonizing suspense. At last they announced the decision. Will would be held until the witness's story could be confirmed.

The next day, we learned that "Roger Travers" had been identified as the escaped convict and taken away to prison in the town of Worcester.

Then, for us, the miracle happened, and Will was set free.

Chapter 6

LAST DAYS

i

That night when we were alone, after all the rejoicing over Will's release, I told him I knew the man calling himself "Roger Travers" was really Stephen Brent.

Will was astonished. "I thought you said he had died?"

"Yes, that's what I believed. What we heard was that the prison released a list of those who had died of plague, and his name was on the list. I still can't believe he's alive."

Will looked thoughtful. Then he said, "That answers something that puzzled me. There was something about the way he spoke about you, Anne. He would drop in little questions about you, without making it sound important. I see now that that's why he came to Stratford, isn't it? His last words to me were that he had found what he came for."

"Yes, it must have been," I said. "Poor Stephen."

"It was decent of him to come forward at his own risk. He is a man of fine character."

The next day, Will wasted no time enlisting George Camden's help.

They went to the Ecclesiastical Court at Worcester, where Stephen had been taken after the trial, and learned that he was in prison under the name Roger Travers, on the charge of escaping from custody twenty-two years ago. George managed to file a petition for the case to be heard.

"I believe we have an excellent chance to get him released," he told us. "The present hierarchy are much more liberal than they were at that date."

A week after Will had at last gone to rejoin his company, George, who had been told of my "friendship" with the man known as Roger Travers, obtained permission for me to visit him in prison in Worcester. I hired a carriage for the four-hour journey and arrived at mid-day. It was a warm summer day, and when I went through the portals of the prison and felt the dankness of those stone walls, my heart contracted with pain that Stephen had put himself here in order to save Will.

We met in a dark room with a small window high in the outside wall. Only a barred opening in the door, where the guard stood outside, broke the solid stone of the walls. If the visitor's room was this grim, I thought, I could only imagine what the prisoners' cells would be like.

When Stephen came in, he gazed at me in astonishment. "Anne! My dear, I cannot believe you are here!"

I held out my hands and he clasped them in his. I looked at the white hair, the lined face, the thin body, so different from the healthy young man I had known, but his voice was the same. "Thank you, thank you for coming."

I said, "We are so grateful for what you did!"

"It was what I had to do. I was still in the town when I heard that your husband had been arrested. Then, when I came to the trial, I saw that no one believed his story."

"But how did you manage to stay hidden?"

"Actually, when I came into the neighborhood, I had looked for Sam Webb. He was my head man at the farm. You may remember him?"

"Sam?" A faint recollection came to me. "Short, stocky man. Good-natured?"

He smiled. "Yes, that's the one. Well, I learned that he had come to live in town, and I approached him cautiously at first. I needn't have worried. He was happy to see me and willing to give me shelter, although he knew he was taking a risk to protect a fugitive. I wanted to find out about you, Anne, and Sam understood the reason without saying a word."

"So where were you when no one could find you?"

Now his smile broadened. "Sam lives in a small house on the street behind Chapel Street. His back garden opens into the narrow lane that passes your garden, about twenty yards along. I slipped out that evening, hearing the sounds of music and voices. Seeing the back gate slightly ajar, I stood listening, and your husband saw me and spoke, just as he said. Then afterward, I quietly went back to Sam's place. When Sam heard the news of the murder and that your husband was accused, I simply stayed on, hoping that it would all be resolved without my help."

"Of course, I see."

I pressed his hand as a heartfelt "Thank you." Then I added in a whisper, "I understand I must not call you Stephen. Can you tell me what happened?"

Speaking softly, he told me his story. "It was true that I did find a priest who came to Margaret as she lay dying, and someone found out and I was arrested. In the prison, I was tossed into a cell with another prisoner, whose name was the one I now bear. We talked, of course, and compared histories. He told me he had also been charged with harboring a priest, one who was passing through his town. He had no family still living, as his parents were long since dead and his wife had died of plague. There were no children. It was much like my own circumstance.

"The plague was sweeping through the prison, and when my friend became infected, I tried to ease his suffering, but within days he was gone. Then they came to take his body away, and when they asked for his name, I told them my own name. There were so many dying that no one cared in the least which of the names in the same cell was correct, and the charges against us were the same."

I looked into his eyes and saw them glistening with tears. "Why did you do that, Stephen?" I whispered.

"You can guess why, can't you, Anne? I knew that I might be in prison for years, and I wanted you to be free. Your life has been good, has it not?"

"Yes, very good. And you were right. I would have waited for you, if I had known."

"Oh, my dear, how glad I am that you were spared that knowledge. I suffered terribly knowing that you were so young, Anne, and that what I did was wrong."

"Don't start all that again, Stephen," I snapped at him as firmly as one can in a whisper. "Enough of that. I loved you to distraction, and it wasn't wrong to me."

He grinned. "I see you're still as spunky as ever."

And we laughed softly together.

Then he said tentatively, "I believe your husband knows about us?"

"Yes."

"I'm glad that he feels no animosity toward me, but I have to say that I am not surprised. I have had the good fortune to find copies of many of his plays, and the man who wrote them is a man of large heart and comprehension of human frailty. He is a brilliant writer and a fine man. I am glad for you, my dear Anne."

It was two weeks later when Stephen was released and

came to tell me goodbye. He was returning to France, which had been his home for so many years. We wrote occasionally for some years, until I had word from his friends there of his death.

After Will's trial, Carla and the Count had wasted no time going home to Italy. Carla had made dramatic declarations of regret that she had been so "mistaken" about seeing Will with the knife in his sleeve.

"Please forgive me," she had sobbed. Nobody forgave her, and I didn't believe for a moment that it was all an innocent mistake. But if not, why did she do it?

One day, Judith asked Will that question. "Papa, why did Carla say she had seen you with the dagger, when we know it wasn't true?"

Will frowned and said nothing for a long moment. Then, "I don't know, Judith. Perhaps—" He broke off and said nothing more. I had asked him the same question and got the same unsatisfactory response.

However, I had a theory about it, and the clue came from Agnes and Susanna. Agnes had said, "When I heard Aunt Carla with Richard that day in her bedroom, I'm sure she saw me going down the stairs and she must have been terrified the Count would find out about it."

And Susanna added, "We know he adored her, but who knows what he might have done if he had known that?"

We had all noticed that Antonio was cool to Richard, but that was no surprise. Nobody else liked Richard either, except maybe Rosanna.

What if Carla was afraid her husband *had* learned about her affair and had killed Richard? After all, the Count was the one who came running out of the garden claiming he had found the body. I had to admit that if anybody had known he had a motive for killing Richard, the Count probably would have been a prime suspect. Carla must have decided to protect her husband by saying she saw Will with the knife.

But was Carla really clever enough to plan this? Not if it was *planned,* I thought. But on the spur of the moment? Yes, it was just the sort of thing she might do.

But why Will? That was easy. She probably *did* see Will through the shrubbery as he walked toward the back of the garden. He was still in his costume, and the image of him carrying a dagger, as he had done in the play, must have sprung to her mind. She couldn't have known her ploy would work, but she probably hoped it would direct attention away from the Count. Then later, she didn't dare to admit what she had done. If Will hadn't been freed, would she have confessed? I wouldn't bet on it.

The authorities hadn't given up on trying to solve the murder. A crown prosecutor had taken over the case, and everyone was questioned over again, but no one was arrested. They had even sent someone to Siena to question the Baldinis. In the end, they appeared to fall back upon the theory that someone had indeed slipped in through the garden gate, seen the dagger, and tracked Richard into the garden. It appeared that we would never know the truth, and I decided that was probably for the best.

About a week after the trial, Rosanna came to the house and found me in my upstairs sitting-room, looking out at the garden. "I need to talk to you, Anne. About Richard."

I nodded, and she went on. "At first, I couldn't believe he was actually dead. Then I felt this great sense of relief, and I was horrified at myself that I should feel that way. It was wrong to be glad someone was dead, but I *was* glad. I had loved him so much when we married, and each time he disappointed me, I forgave him, because I didn't want to lose his affection. When he demanded money, I thought it was only right that he should have what was mine, but when it came to David's money, I had to resist."

She looked at me as if appealing for approval, and I told her she was quite right.

"When he was violent to me and even to Agnes," she went on, "I believed him when he said it would never happen again. But then, when Agnes told me he and Carla were making love, I pretended that I didn't believe it. I never told you this, Anne, but *I did believe it.* I had suspected sometimes that when he was away from Stratford, he saw other women, but this was in my own home, and with my dear cousin. I could not forgive that!"

I said softly, "What about Carla? She was also guilty, wasn't she?"

"Yes, she was very wrong, too. But it's always the man who makes the overtures, isn't it?"

I wouldn't count on that, I thought.

"You remember, Anne, how Agnes kept saying how she *hated* Richard, and I discovered that that was how I felt too. I actually *hated* him. My own husband!"

I could easily have told her she had plenty of reason to hate Richard, but it wasn't logic she wanted. Rosanna's nature was so gentle, so loving, that I felt what she needed was to forgive herself for having such feelings, and that would come with time.

I told Agnes later something of what her mother had said, and she was glad to know that Rosanna was not grieving over Richard, as Agnes had feared, and thus would not hate the person who had killed Richard.

About that same time, I remembered that there was a question I had wanted to ask Tom Quiney on the day I had found him with the sexton digging the grave for his father.

Now I was aware that Tom had been acting strangely since the day of the murder. At the play, he had not sat near either Adrian or his father, nor even with Uncle Nate. In the evening, at the reception, he had seemed nervous and distressed. That would be natural enough when it was his father who was murdered. Yet something in his manner puzzled me. Now, a week had gone by since the trial, and we had seen no sign of him.

I walked along the river to the church, looking for him, only to be told by the sexton that Tom had not been back on his job since the day they were digging the grave.

"Poor lad," he said. "He ain't been here with me, but he's been inside betimes."

I went into the church and walked down the nave, but saw no sign of Tom. Then I looked into a side chapel, and there he was, not on his knees, as I had half expected, but sitting with his head bent. I noticed his hands were clenched, and when I spoke to him, he jumped up and stared at me wildly.

"What is it, Tom?" I asked softly.

"Oh, it's you, Anne."

I brought him back to the house and put some food in front of him, which he ate ravenously. When he had finished, I said, "Something is troubling you, isn't it, Tom?"

"Yes. I don't know what to do."

"Has it anything to do with your Uncle Nate?"

"Well, partly."

Now was the time for my question. "Tom, do you remember the day you told me about seeing your father with Libby Russell at her house?"

He nodded.

"Did you tell anyone else about it?"

"You said not to, but I did tell just one person. I told Uncle Nate."

"Was he very angry?"

"Oh, yes. He said my father was a wicked, wicked man."

"And when someone killed your father that night, did you wonder—were you afraid—?"

"That it might be Uncle Nate?"

"Yes, I suppose I did wonder."

"Is this what has been troubling you, Tom?"

"I wouldn't like it to be Uncle, but no, it's not that. It's the other thing. I can't take it in. It can't be true, but I guess it is."

"What is that, Tom?"

"It's about my money. What I inherited from my grandfather."

"Yes. You are going to buy a farm?"

"I would have. But it's gone."

"How can that be?"

"There's what they call a mercantile house, that holds money and keeps it until you need it, and I went there the very day before the play at Guild Hall, because I wanted to find out how much I had, and the man told me there was nothing left. My father had taken all the money!"

I said there must be some mistake, and we went directly to George Camden's office to ask for his help.

George came back and learned to his dismay that Richard had deposited the money in his own name as well as his son's, and over time, he had withdrawn various large sums, until in the end, it was gone.

I was appalled, but was it really surprising? If Richard had access to any money, he couldn't leave it alone, even money belonging to his own son.

Now Tom turned for consolation to Nate Fletcher,

spending much of his time with him, although there was no talk now about buying a farm. His whole young life was turned awry not merely by the loss of his fortune but more painfully by the disillusion of Richard's betrayal.

ii

Our lives had gone back to what was normal for us. That is, Will went back to London, wrote plays, and helped run his company, while I carried on in Stratford. Only a few months had passed when Will came home again. I had to admit he did come more often and stayed longer than in the early days.

Soon after he arrived, we received a shock. A letter from Italy came for Will one morning as we sat at the breakfast table. The servant handed Will a packet, wrapped and sealed, with an inscription that it was "to be opened by William Shakespeare only."

"Why all the secrecy?" Will muttered, as he broke the seals. "It's from the Count." He read quickly through the letter, then handed it to me without a word.

My dear Shakespeare,

You will perhaps be surprised at what I have to say to you. I must ask you to keep this in a safe place, and not to reveal its contents at present to anyone other than to your wife, if it is your wish for her to read it.

I am the person who killed Richard Quiney. I have made confession to my priest, and now I must make certain that no one else will be convicted for this crime. I know the police are still questioning many others, and I entrust this to you to prevent another person being accused, if for any reason I should be unable to intercede in person.

You may ask, why did I permit you to be tried for the crime which I knew you did not commit? I can assure you, my dear friend, that I should have stepped forward if you had been found guilty. I was exactly on the point of speaking out at the trial when the old gentleman appeared and so wonderfully saved you from that fate.

You will wish to know why I did this thing. There were two reasons why I detested the abominable Richard Quiney. My dear wife had told me that her cousin's husband had attempted to make love to her. She of course refused him, and I hated him for this, but I could understand. My wife is a very beautiful woman, and it is but natural that a man should make such an attempt. However, she is virtuous, and I should not have committed murder on that account.

No, the reason lies elsewhere. When my wife's cousin, Edward Bushell, told me the story of Richard's betrayal of our cause, I knew from that moment that I should have my revenge upon him. I watched him each day, waiting for my opportunity. It was late on that evening at your party when I saw Richard walking out into the garden. I was standing in the library, and I saw the jeweled dagger lying on the table by the window. I seized it and followed him, taking a path to one side of the one he had taken. I saw him turn and cross the garden to the corner by the linden tree, and it was there I confronted him. He laughed and said whatever he had done didn't matter, as the rebellion was never going to succeed anyhow. At this, I was seized with fury, and when he turned to walk away, I pulled the dagger from the sheath and stabbed him. Had he been a true gentleman, I should not have struck him in the back, but for a traitor, I did not hesitate. The knife was very sharp, as we all had seen, and he did not cry out. He simply fell forward. I threw the dagger and the sheath on the ground. I bent over to make sure he was dead. Then I walked slowly back toward the house, calling out for help as I came to the terrace.

My dear Lotta knows nothing of this. She is fanciful, as we know, and she truly believes she saw you in the garden. She regrets this much, and I trust you will forgive her for her mistake and forgive me for not stepping forward sooner.

Thank you for receiving this. I have made my peace with God.

The letter was signed with a flourish which I made out to be "Antonio Baldini."

I laid the letter on the table and looked at Will. "I'm sure you'll forgive his dear little wife for her mistake."

Will snorted. "His *virtuous* little wife. Poor chap—he really believes that!"

I nodded. "Now I see why Antonio tried to assure me that you wouldn't be convicted of the murder."

"Yes, and I see now that at the trial, he made a great point of seeing me coming from the *opposite* end of the garden and walking *slowly,* implying that I hadn't just committed a murder."

So, now, what should Will do?

"Of course, it's my duty to report this to the court." His voice was solemn, but the corner of his lip was curled in a grin. "But I'll be damned if I do it. The Count is hardly a threat to society. If this came from someone who might kill again, it would be different."

And so we agreed to put the letter in our lock box and say nothing to a living soul, and Will wrote accordingly to Antonio. It was enough that we knew who had killed Richard.

I thought how ironic it was that I had actually guessed the truth, and that if my theory was correct, Carla had instinctively guessed too that her husband had killed Richard and that was why she invented the story about Will. At least, I no longer had to worry that our friends, or worse still, any member of our family, might have been guilty of the crime.

There were still things about the crime that we didn't know. One day, Will asked George Camden what had become of the gold coin they had found in Richard's hand when his body was brought in from the garden. George gave a sheepish grin and said he had forgotten it until he found it days later in his pocket. At that point, he had decided it could not help Will's case, so he had simply put it away and later had given it to Rosanna, without saying where it came from.

When Will got back to writing again, he continued in the vein of the charming *Much Ado About Nothing*, a comedy which had been performed before the tragic events of the treason. The witty Beatrice and Benedick, battling their way to reluctant matrimony, were now followed by *Twelfth Night*, for me the most delightful of Will's comedies. The charming young ladies, Viola and Olivia, survive all the disguises and mistaken identities and end up happily married to their chosen swains. Only Malvolio, in his yellow stockings and his crossed garters, remains impervious to the fun.

Weddings were in the air in real life as well that year. Susanna and Dr. John Hall were first.

Next came Agnes, whose Oxford Don, Charles Grey,

had been awarded a Fellowship, making it possible for him to marry, and Stratford was near enough for mutual visits with Rosanna.

In the following year, Will's new play, *Macbeth*, about the Scottish King who murdered his way to the throne, was due to open at the Globe Theater. We all went to London for the occasion—the two young married couples, and Rosanna and I with Judith and David, who, inspired by their elder siblings, had become engaged.

Everyone loved the play, and when we were back in Stratford, the young husbands joined in the family custom of performing skits and pantomimes, from Will's plays or others. Now we had hilarious scenes of the three witches around the cauldron, and spooky ones at the dining table when Macbeth sees the ghost of Banquo in his chair, and of course everyone's favorite, with Judith, our leading actress, as Lady Macbeth, walking in her sleep and wringing her hands.

iii

The year 1603 brought some dramatic events. It began with the death of Queen Elizabeth on the 19th day of March. Will had never forgiven the Queen for what he saw as her cruelty at the time of the treason. Even though at the last moment she had spared the life of his young Earl, he still loathed the very sound of her name, with the result that he, alone among poets and statesmen, never wrote a word of praise at her death.

Then the great news came. King James VI of Scotland became James I of England, and within two weeks of his accession, he freed the Earl of Southampton from the Tower, along with many of the former conspirators.

A few months later, I received a note from the young Countess of Southampton, inviting Will and me to join them at Titchfield, where a few friends would gather to celebrate her husband's freedom from prison.

Titchfield! Their country seat in Hampshire where Will had gone so long ago and encountered his first experience of life among the rich and titled. Now he would go as an old and trusted friend of the Earl and I as the "mother figure" of my first encounter with the pretty little pregnant Lady-in-Waiting to the Queen.

On the journey, now in a comfortable carriage, I had time to reflect on all the recent events in our lives. Lulled to drowsiness by the motion of the carriage, words and phrases floated on my consciousness.

Why was Carla so pouty and sulky in the few days before the Count arrived in Stratford?

Why was Will so reluctant to answer when asked why Carla said she saw him in the garden with the dagger when we all knew it wasn't true? Usually so quick to respond, to express possible reasons for events, Will had sat silent, staring into space.

Then I could hear the Count occasionally calling his wife "Lotta" when everyone else called her "Carla." Rosanna had explained that her cousin's name was Carlotta, but she had always been called Carla until she married, and the Count liked "Lotta" as his pet name for her.

And what about the gold coin in Richard's hand when the body was brought into the house? There was something about that that didn't make sense, but I couldn't quite think what it was.

Then I would doze off and think of the visit to come. There were some questions I wanted to ask the Earl, if I had the chance.

iv

The size and grandeur of Titchfield was impressive, and our host greeted us warmly. Will knew many of the guests, but I didn't, and I was often at the mercy of titled ladies who were less than cordial.

One day, I heard from across the room the voice of a Duchess, who obviously didn't care if she was overheard, saying, "Oh, she is the wife of that actor fellow."

Her companion said, "Wasn't he the one who wrote those sonnets that we passed about among ourselves?"

"Yes, I believe he was. Quite juicy, weren't they?" And they giggled like young girls, although it had been many years since that time.

I wasn't offended. After all, it was the way of the world. If I had been a Duchess, would I have been any different? Who knows? And her remark reminded me of something I wanted to know.

The Countess herself was cordial. We talked of the days when she was Lady Elizabeth Vernon, and we laughed over the story of my being followed that day in London when I left her, after delivering the message from the Earl about when they would be married.

On the last day of our visit, I had the chance I been hoping for and found the young Earl on the terrace. He greeted me warmly and suggested we walk in the garden, where he mused on the past. "It was some ten years ago that William was here for the first time, was it not? And I was not yet twenty, and a child with not a serious thought in my head. Now I am having my thirtieth birthday soon, and I am an old man beyond my years."

I said, "You have had experiences that might age anyone."

"Exactly." A sad, sweet smile lighted his face. "Years in prison with no hope of a future may do that indeed. Now, what is it you want to ask me?"

I laughed. "How did you know?"

Again that captivating smile. "If I were in your place, I should wonder about the past."

I seized my chance. "Well then, when Will was here that first time, he wrote many sonnets. Did everyone read them?"

"Yes, we passed them about among ourselves, and everyone was delighted with their cleverness and their marvelous poetry. But in the end, he wrote some unkind things about a young woman named Lotta, and she was very angry."

I felt a little thrill of triumph that one of my questions had been answered without my having to ask.

I smiled. "I have read them, and I can understand she would not be pleased."

We went on to speak of his wife and child, and he expressed his gratitude for Will's loyalty during the time of troubles and his relief that Will had not suffered as a result. Then we chatted about Will's plays as we moved back toward the house.

Will and I went back to London together, and I said nothing during the drive, but when we reached his lodgings and were settled in and had our dinner sent up, I looked him in the eye.

"All right, Will, why didn't you tell me you had known Carla before?"

He grinned. "I thought you would find that out. But does it really matter now?"

"Certainly not in the way you think, but you might have trusted me. Did you always know, from the first time I mentioned her name?"

"Oh, no, Anne. I would at least have admitted to having met her. I didn't know who she was until the night of the murder, when Rosanna introduced me to her at our party after the performance of *Julius Caesar*. I looked into her face as she made a mocking curtsey to me, and I thought at first it was only a resemblance. Then I realized it was the same woman. You see, I had known her only as 'Lotta,' not as 'Carla.' "

"The dark lady of your sonnets?"

"Yes. Oh, lord, the last thing I ever wanted was to see her again. It brought back all that period of youthful madness. I thought of telling you at once, but I saw no point in bringing it up. I was sure she would not tell you, because she felt I had humiliated her and she would never want to reveal that. Besides, her husband knew nothing whatever about her activities, and she certainly didn't want him to know. Poor fellow, believing she was a 'virtuous' woman. She was there at Titchfield only a short time and she never spoke of her life. I knew nothing about her."

"There's something I've never told you, Will. That night at the party, I saw you and Carla in the anteroom. I followed her and stood across the passage in the doorway where I could see but not hear. I can't say I was proud of myself for spying. What was she saying to you?"

"She said she knew I must still love her, in spite of everything, and she wanted us to be 'together again,' as she put it, after the Count had gone back to Italy. She put her arms around my neck, and when I more or less pushed her away, she was furious. She couldn't seem to believe that I didn't want her."

Back in Stratford, I was still sorting out my feelings about learning that silly Carla was the brunette lady of Will's sonnets. She certainly had never mentioned Will nor shown any interest in hearing about him, in spite of his celebrity. It was not until she finally met him at the party that she approached him. Oh, well, I felt pretty sure we had seen the last of Carla.

But no such luck. In the summer, Rosanna heard the sad news that the Count had died, and a distraught Carla soon arrived and threw herself sobbing on her cousin. Needless to say, Rosanna took her in and looked after her. We learned then that the Count had been ailing for some time and his doctors had been concerned.

I wondered if the illness might have been coming on for longer than they knew. Wasn't it likely that when the Count wrote his letter of confession to Will, he wanted to be sure it was sent before he might have a fatal illness?

Within a month, Carla seemed to have recovered her usual spirits and behaved toward all of us as if she had forgotten about Richard's murder and even about the death of her husband. Agnes was indignant, but Rosanna said Carla was like a child and she couldn't send her away.

Then I began to wonder about the Count's confession. Was there something about it that didn't quite ring true? I began putting together in my mind the questions that had been bothering me about the whole matter of Richard's murder.

I had been reading *Hamlet* again, my favorite of all Will's plays at the time, and it had suggested to me a way of finding some answers to my questions. I had formed a number of theories, and had finally come to a decision.

There were several possibilities, but there was no way to prove any one of them. Or so I thought until I was reminded by *Hamlet* that there might be a way.

A family skit would be my best chance.

Accordingly, I announced that next evening on the terrace we would have three pantomimes. Our custom was for one of us to select one of Will's plays or sometimes a play by another author and organize the skits from that play. This time, I said, our source would be an old play that had once been popular before Will's day. There would be no lines to speak. It would be entirely in silent action.

The weather began the day with rain but cleared up beautifully by evening. About nine o'clock, it was dusk, so that the garden was just visible but partially dark. I had placed my "audience" in a sort of double crescent along the terrace, facing the garden. I put Carla in the center, with Rosanna, John, and Mary on her left. On her right were Agnes and her husband, John Grey, with Susanna and her husband at the end. In the second row were Rosanna's son David, Nate Fletcher, Tom Quiney, and Edward Bushell. I had decided to use the actual shrubs and trees in the garden for my stage setting, supplemented by a few props which were brought as needed by two of our young servants. My "cast members" had all rehearsed their parts earlier, and were ready to begin.

I held up a sign saying, "Pantomime One, in Three Parts."

As the skit opens, Susanna walks over to a long bench, lies down on it, and feigns falling asleep. Then a tall, handsome young man (played by her husband Dr. Hall, wearing a wig of reddish wavy hair), comes and stands looking down at her. Then he bends over, taking her in his arms, clearly expressing passionate love for her, and she responds. (The doctor had joked that this role didn't require much acting on his part.)

Now, David enters from the back, portraying a shy young man. He carries an armful of flowers, and when he turns and sees the couple, he stops, looks horrified, drops the flowers, and runs away.

The actors leave the stage, and I signal to my "prop men" to bring out several tied stalks of wheat, leaning them against a tree.

Now we see a stocky, middle-aged man, played by George Camden, standing in a "wheat field."

David, the young man with the flowers in the previous scene, approaches the older man (obviously a farmer) and begins to tell him something. The farmer is shocked, then enraged, and, raising his fist in wildly threatening gestures, he dashes off.

Now, we see again the tall, red-haired young man who had made love to the girl on the bench. He is standing in the garden, in a dell visible to the audience, and the older man approaches him, waving his arms and exhibiting extreme fury. The younger man smiles, shrugs, and turns his back.

Then the farmer reaches into his sleeve and pulls out a dagger with a jeweled handle (not as sparkling as the one that had killed Richard, but the best I had found to use as a prop). As he raises it toward the back of the younger man, Nate Fletcher leaped to his feet, shouting, "Here, what's this? Is that supposed to be me there?"

Tom Quiney pulled Nate's arm. "It's only a play, Uncle Nate. It isn't real."

Looking embarrassed, Nate sat down, grunting about "nonsense."

Next came "Pantomime Two." We had managed to

"borrow" a very fashionable vest and coat belonging to Edward Bushell, which fit Agnes's husband, Charles Grey, perfectly. In this dandified outfit, Charles appears, facing the tall young man in the reddish wig. They are obviously quarreling, when someone walks past them carrying a banner which says "TRAITOR!" The Bushell character points to the Richard character and shows great anger.

Then the scene shifts to the same dell in the garden seen before, and the Bushell character brings out a jeweled dagger, the same one used in the first pantomime, and raises it toward the back of the Richard character.

Everyone turned toward Edward, who looked puzzled and finally said irritably, "Well, is that all? I don't understand. Why is the fellow wearing my coat? I see it all has something to do with Richard's death, but I'd much rather have one of Will's plays."

Susanna and I exchanged glances. Was Edward really clever, or was he just dense?

For my third pantomime, I had a cast of three. The doctor was still playing the tall man with the wavy red hair. George Camden now wore a wig of thick dark hair liberally streaked with gray. Judith, our leading actress, would play the lady, wearing an elegant red gown with ruffled cuffs at her wrists, and a tiara of diamonds on her dark hair.

As the action begins, the lady seems to be pleading with the tall, red-haired man, who shakes his head and starts to walk away. She calls him back, and now he listens and nods his head.

The older man with graying hair stands back of a bush, watching, but unseen by the other two.

Next, we see the dark-haired lady waiting in the little dell that is screened by shrubs but can be seen by the audience. George, as the older man, is nowhere to be seen. The red-haired man approaches and joins the lady. She is clearly angry and shakes her fist at the man. Then she smiles and puts her face up to his. He bends and kisses her lightly, then turns away. They appear to argue, and then she shows him a bright gold coin. He looks at it and shakes his head, no. The lady furiously tosses the coin onto the ground behind the man. He bends over, his back to her, and picks up the coin. At that moment, she pulls out the jeweled dagger from her right sleeve, tosses the sheath on the ground, and raising her left arm, stabs him in the back. As he falls face down to the ground, we see the silver-haired man approach and pull back a tall shrub, just in time to see the man lying on the ground and to see the lady running away.

I had been watching Carla and had seen the fear on her face from the beginning. Now she looked with absolute terror at the scene in the garden.

Then, with a scream of anguish, she leaped to her feet and ran into the house. We could hear her footsteps pounding through the parlor and into the hall, and then the heavy door in the entry, which had been left partially open because of the heat, was slammed shut.

My three cast members already knew the purpose of my pantomime, and now everyone else except John and Mary, who were totally bewildered, had begun to put together the significance of Carla's terror. The men agreed at once to spread out and search for her, especially along the river, as we were afraid that might be where she would go. Agnes said she would take her mother home and stay with her, as Aunt Carla would surely come back there, and Edward went with them.

I soothed John and Mary and saw them upstairs to their bedroom. Then I sank down on a chair by the window in my upstairs sitting room, overlooking the front of the house. The windows were open, and a soft breeze came off the river.

Would Carla really throw herself into the Avon? I felt pangs of guilt that I hadn't anticipated. Poor Carla! She was so childish and probably not fully developed in her mind. I had wanted so much to know if my guess was correct. Had I been wrong to do this?

Suddenly I heard a voice at my back. "Hello, Anne."

I turned and saw Carla staring at me with a look of rage that made me shudder.

I said, "We thought you had gone out."

"Yes, that's what I wanted you to think. I slammed the door and then I hid behind the sofa in the anteroom. I heard them all going out to look for me. Then I crept out and went into the parlor and then I came up the stairs looking for you. Wasn't I clever?"

"Yes, very clever, Carla."

"And now we are here alone, Anne. And you are going to pay for what you did."

With a quick motion, she reached into her right sleeve and pulled out the jeweled dagger in its sheath.

"This was in its case in the parlor, so easy for anyone to pick it up." Her eyes glittered with hatred. "You think you are so far above poor little Carla. You and brainy Will with his poems and his plays. But he once loved me, more than he ever cared for an old woman like you!"

I tried soothing murmurs. "Yes, Carla, I know he did. You are beautiful. And Antonio loved you dearly. Think of him, Carla. He would not want you to commit another crime, would he?"

If I thought this would soften her, I was wrong. Not a tremor.

Her voice was hoarse. "You are a devil, Anne. You

brought them all back to life, there in the garden! How did you know I killed Richard?"

Then I saw the madness in her eyes. The figures in the pantomime were real to her, just as the ghosts of past lovers were real to her, just as Will as the ghost of Julius Caesar had been real to her. No wonder the Count had been so protective. He knew her fantasies were more than mere foolishness.

I decided to try a little flattery. "But Carla, wasn't Richard in love with you? Why did you kill him?"

"He told me I was so beautiful, he couldn't resist me. And then, when Agnes heard us together, he said it must stop. He did not want Rosanna to know. I was so angry. How could he care more for her than for me?"

"Is that why you were offering him money?"

"Of course. I told him to meet me under the elm tree. When he came, I said I would stay after my husband went home and we could be together again. I knew he needed money, so I gave him a gold coin worth very much money. But he laughed at me and said he had never loved me but he wouldn't mind taking my money. When he bent over to pick up the coin I pulled the dagger out and plunged it into his back and he fell forward without a sound. You see, it is so easy. Look!"

Now she pulled the dagger from its sheath and started to move toward me. I could feel my heart thudding, and I looked around wildly for any weapon I could seize. There was a small bronze statue on a nearby table, and I snatched it up, feeling its puny weight. If I got close enough to her to strike her with it, it would be too late to avoid the dagger.

Instead, I threw it at her with all my strength, but she saw my intent and jumped aside, laughing as it struck the marble floor. Then I ran across the room, standing behind a large sofa, but she leaped up onto the sofa and raised the dagger above me, slashing down toward my head. I dodged to the side, and I saw the slice from that sharp blade as it cut into the cushion of the sofa. Now I came round the end of the sofa and threw myself at her feet, pulling her to the floor.

Still clutching the dagger, she tried again to bring it down on me. I reached for her left wrist and gave it a twist, and the dagger flew across the floor. Both of us were lying flat, and we crawled across the slippery marble toward where it lay. Carla was closer to it, and as she reached for it, I managed to get to my feet and kick it swiftly out of her grasp. Then I tried to stamp on her hand but she was too quick for me. She got to her feet in a flash and started toward me, howling with rage, and we both made a dash toward where the dagger lay in the doorway at the top of the stairs.

Pain gripped my chest as I gasped for breath, and I could hear Carla panting, when suddenly George Camden appeared in the doorway. For a moment I didn't recognize him, as he was still wearing the wig of black hair streaked with gray he had worn in the pantomime. He stared at us in amazement. Then he bent and picked up the dagger, holding it gingerly, with its sharp blade exposed, and seeing the sheath on the floor near the window, he walked over, picked it up, and carefully put the blade back inside.

Now I noticed that Carla had stopped all motions of animosity toward me and was standing as if frozen, staring at George where he stood with his back to the window. Then she cried out "Antonio!" and ran toward him, throwing herself into his arms.

It didn't take George long to grasp the situation. I took the dagger from him and put it on a high shelf, while he held Carla firmly to his chest. Over her head, he said softly to me, "She tried . . . ?" And I nodded.

Now Carla was sobbing and pouring out her hatred of me and how glad she was that Antonio had come to save her. Finally the tears subsided, and she pulled back and gazed up into George's face.

Then, with a cry of horror, she drew back. "You are not Antonio! Where is he? My darling, where are you? I know you are somewhere. . . ."

George stepped toward her and tried to soothe her, but she turned and glared at me with the same look of madness I had seen before.

"You tried to fool me, you devil, but Antonio is dead, isn't he? I want to be with him. I know he is waiting for me."

And without a moment's hesitation, she ran to the window and threw herself out onto the paving stones thirty feet below.

V

By the time Will came back to Stratford, Carla's body had been sent back to Siena to be placed beside her husband in the family vault, and life had gradually gone back to its usual tempo.

When Will heard about the pantomimes, he said. " 'The play's the thing to catch the conscience of the King!' "

"Yes," I said, "it worked for Hamlet, why not for us?"

"So why did you do the first two skits?"

"Well, I thought it probably was Carla, but it was only a guess, and what if I had been wrong and it was Nate or Edward after all? I thought it might be a good idea to try them out. Nate was outraged at Richard for seducing his beloved Libby, and he must equally have hated Richard for what he did to poor Tom, robbing the boy of his fortune, but worse than that, of his need to love his father. However, he subsided so meekly when Tom assured him it was only make-believe that I knew, with Nate's temper, that if he had been guilty, he would have raved on about his hatred of Richard and given himself away."

"And what about Edward?"

"I had to conclude that he was so frightened by the dagger that the idea of anyone believing that he could actually stab Richard was beyond his imagining. He is truly a timid rabbit."

"So, what put you onto Carla as the guilty party?"

"Well, first I had to ask why should she kill *Richard?* Plenty of people might have wanted to. Besides Edward and Nate, Agnes and David, his stepchildren, hated him, and Susanna and Judith shared their anger at Richard's behavior. There was Edward, of course. And even Rosanna had finally turned against Richard. George had a legal run-in with Richard, as well as being furious at his treatment of Rosanna.

"The problem was, I couldn't believe any of these people could have committed a murder. But of all the people concerned, Carla seemed to me to be the one person who *wouldn't* kill Richard. And she is small in stature. I couldn't see how she could stab him in the back. At the same time, she was the type who would have no scruples if something displeased her. I had always thought she was somewhat unbalanced in her mind. The irrational belief in ghosts, her easily detected lovemaking with Richard in her cousin's own home, were not the acts of a normal person.

"Then I wondered, why was she so sulky just before the Count came to Stratford? Had Richard broken off their little romance when Agnes caught them in the act? And of course that proved to be true.

"Then, why did Carla try to implicate you in the murder? Was there some reason she disliked you? Had you met before? Then at the party, I saw her follow you down the hall into the anteroom, and I saw just enough to gather that she was flirting with you, in her usual fashion, and that you were definitely refusing her. I didn't hang about to see any more.

"I also thought about the relationship between the Count's family and the Southamptons. Then, when Judith asked you why Carla claimed she saw you with the dagger, you were plainly reluctant to talk about it. An idea formed in my mind, and when we went to Titchfield, the Earl told me about the young lady named Lotta who was a guest at Titchfield and had been humiliated by your sonnets. The pattern was there of a woman who cannot bear rejection and carries her resentment forever.

"And, as if to confirm my suspicion of her, I noticed for the first time that Carla used her left hand regularly. It's not something you notice unless there's a reason, and I remembered how at the trial she had promptly pointed to her right arm when asked which of your sleeves had the dagger in it."

Now Will interrupted for the first time. "So how did you account for the Count's letter of confession? Didn't you believe him?"

"Certainly I did, at the time. All this came later. But when all these vague ideas began to take form, it was that letter that convinced me I was on the right track."

"The Count's letter?"

"Yes. It was what was *not* there that struck me. He gave

a detailed account of how he committed the murder, *but he said nothing about the gold coin in Richard's hand.* Someone must have offered the coin to Richard. He certainly didn't have any money of that value. *But the Count didn't know about it.*"

Will pondered. "I see. Yes, I remember now. When Richard's body was brought in and placed on the table, the Count had left the room to go and look for his precious Carla. That's when I found the coin in Richard's hand and gave it to George. And that could also explain why Richard was stabbed in the back, and how even a small woman like Carla could have done it. She tosses the coin at him and he bends over to pick it up, and that's her chance."

"Exactly! That's how I did the pantomime, and it proved to be right. The Count came in sight of them just as Richard fell, but he hadn't seen the gold coin because it was already in Richard's hand."

Will frowned. "In the Count's letter, he sounded very convincing when he wrote of hating Richard and wanting revenge for the betrayal of their cause. Was that just invented?"

"I wondered about that, too. What I think may have happened is that Antonio really did feel that way and perhaps when he came to Stratford and saw Richard there, he may have felt all his anger return and may have had a passionate desire to kill Richard if the chance presented itself. So, when he put that forth as his motive in his letter to you, it made a most believable scenario to him. It was almost as if someone else had got there before him. But then, to his horror, he believed it might have been his precious Carla who did it."

Will said, "Yes, I agree. What do we know about the Count's death, Anne? Was he ill for some time?"

"Yes. Carla was rather vague about it, but Rosanna learned that for a long time, he had complained of pains in his chest."

"Isn't it likely that he knew he was dying when he sent me that letter? He wanted to protect his precious little wife if she should ever be suspected of Richard's murder."

"Yes. That seemed to be the reason for his confession, but you see, I couldn't be really sure. I guessed that he didn't actually *see* her commit the murder. He came along just as she was running away and *believed* that she had done it."

In the end, Carla's death was reported as a tragic accident and no further questions were asked. I expected Rosanna to grieve over her cousin, but she surprised me by announcing that she had never forgiven Carla for her affair with Richard. Rosanna was horrified that Carla had tried to kill me, and she never spoke of her cousin again.

A year later, Rosanna began inviting George to little dinners at her place, and thus encouraged, he finally asked her to marry him and was repaid for all his years of silent devotion.

For the next ten years, Will continued to produce plays of incomparable greatness, among them the tragedies of *King Lear*, *Othello*, and others. This period culminated in the magic of *The Tempest*, for me the most delightful of all his comedies, and the play that proved to be his last.

Tragedy then came into our lives, for within a year of the writing of *The Tempest*, Will's mind began to fail. The decline was gradual but unmistakable. His memory faded. He came home to live in Stratford and never returned to London, forgetting much of his life there.

When it came time to write his will, the clerk had to write it for him, as his hand shook with palsy. But there was one item he requested. In his quavering voice, he said, "Put in that my wife should have my second-best bed."

That brought a lump to my throat, remembering the time long ago when we were furnishing the grand rooms at New Place. He had ordered the finest bed for John and Mary, and we had often joked about ours being the "second-best." Now, out of all his hazy recollections, Will remembered that.

When the end came, and the family and friends grieved for him, and hundreds of people throughout the realm mourned for him, I remembered that lad of eighteen, so brilliant, so full of vitality, who had lavished his affection on me and filled my life with joy.

And so, on that day in April, in the year 1616, when he was laid to rest in Holy Trinity Church, I knelt at his gravestone and whispered Horatio's farewell words to Hamlet: "May flights of angels sing thee to thy rest."

Afterword

For readers who may want to know "what's true and what isn't," I recommend Ian Wilson's SHAKESPEARE: THE EVIDENCE (St. Martin's Press, 1993), which is a reliable and delightfully readable source for what is known of Shakespeare's life.

About the Author

Audrey Peterson fell in love with England when, as Professor of English at California State University at Long Beach, she traveled there to pursue research for scholarly publication, so it is no surprise that all of her mystery novels are set in England. After a series of novels about American academics in Britain, she turned to the Victorian period in *An Unmourned Death* (Five Star Publishing, 2002), featuring a young woman who works for a private detective agency in London in the 1880s. Now, in *Murder in Stratford,* she weaves a fascinating tale of murder and intrigue in the life of William Shakespeare, as "told" by his wife Anne.

After living for some years in Bellingham, Washington, where her late husband was on the faculty at Western Washington University, Audrey now makes her home in Huntington Beach, California, near her daughters and two grandchildren.